Praise for

A WHOLE NOTHER STORY

"If Lemony Snicket and Dave Barry got married and had a baby, this book would be it." —Critiquing the World

"If the kids are waiting for the next Wimpy Kid book, hand them this one. —*San Francisco Chronicle*

★ "A grand escapade centered around a close family of smart, helpful, likable characters who run into all sorts of oddball wanderers on the road and show plenty of inner stuff when push comes to shove. . . . Great fun." —*Kirkus Reviews,* starred review

"My favorite part? The WHOLE BOOK!" —Kent, grade 6

"The storytelling, which merges deadpan narration with an absurdist sense of humor, is the real star of this fast-paced adventure." —*Publishers Weekly*

"A rare find. Its tone is light and amusing, and the jokes honestly never seem to end. . . . The type of jesting here is reminiscent of humorous authors like Lemony Snicket and Shel Silverstein." —Kidsreads.com

"A little word of advice: THIS BOOK ROCKS!" —Rose, grade 5

"Horizon-expanding wordplay, quirky characters, laugh-out-loud turns-of-phrase, and triskaidekamania. . . . Readers or listeners will enjoy the ride and will look forward to the Cheesmans' future adventures." —*Booklist*

"Dr. Cuthbert Soup has the prescription for humor in *A Whole Nother Story,* which is laugh-out-loud funny." —*The Missourian*

Books by the one and only
DR. CUTHBERT SOUP

A Whole Nother Story
Another Whole Nother Story

A WHOLE NOTHER STORY

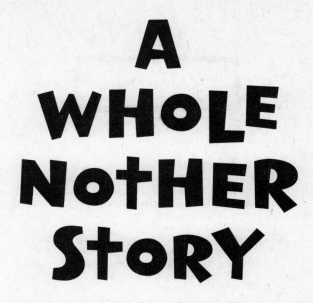

Dr. Cuthbert Soup

illustrations by

Jeffrey Stewart Timmins

BLOOMSBURY

NEW YORK BERLIN LONDON SYDNEY

For Andrea Marie

First published in the United States of America in January 2010
by Bloomsbury Books for Young Readers
Paperback edition published in September 2010
www.bloomsburykids.com

For information about permission to reproduce selections from this book, write to
Permissions, Bloomsbury BFYR, 175 Fifth Avenue, New York, New York 10010

The Library of Congress has cataloged the hardcover edition as follows:
Soup, Cuthbert.
A whole nother story / by Cuthbert Soup ; illustrations by Jeffrey Stewart Timmins. — 1st U.S. ed.
p.   cm.
Summary: Ethan Cheeseman and his children, ages eight, twelve, and fourteen, hope to
settle in a nice small town, at least long enough to complete work on a time machine, but spies
and government agents have been pursuing them for two years and are about to catch up.
ISBN 978-1-59990-435-1 (hardcover)
[1. Inventions—Fiction. 2. Spies—Fiction. 3. Family life—Fiction. 4. Moving, Household—Fiction.
5. Automobile travel—Fiction. 6. Humorous stories.] I. Timmins, Jeffrey Stewart, ill. II. Title.
PZ7.C97Who 2010   [Fic]—dc22   2009021998

ISBN 978-1-59990-518-1 (paperback)

Book design by Donna Mark
Typeset by Westchester Book Composition
Printed in the U.S.A. by Quad/Graphics Fairfield, Pennsylvania
3 5 7 9 10 8 6 4 2

All papers used by Bloomsbury Publishing, Inc., are natural, recyclable products
made from wood grown in well-managed forests. The manufacturing processes
conform to the environmental regulations of the country of origin.

"The pen is mightier than the sword, though both can ruin a good shirt."

DR. CUTHBERT SOUP, ADVISOR TO THE ILL-ADVISED

A LITTLE ADVICE

If I could give you all just one word of advice, it would be . . . well, an incomplete sentence. Besides being grammatically iffy, I'm sure you'd agree that a single word of advice is rarely of much use. Even the phrase "Look out!" (which could prove to be life-saving advice—especially where large falling objects or missing manhole covers are concerned) is two words.

To simply shout out "Look!" to a friend as a tuba falls from a ninth-story window toward his unsuspecting head will, at best, only serve to make sure he gets a good look at the tuba before it parades him, unceremoniously, into the sidewalk.

And so, throughout this book, I will attempt to offer more than one word of wisdom whether you want it or not because, after all, that is what we do here at the National Center for Unsolicited Advice.

However, I will at the same time try not to be too overbearing because, as we all know, no one likes a busybody. It seems as though every time you turn around (and believe me, you turn around a lot more often than you might think), someone is telling you how to do or how not to do something. Parents, teachers, classmates, bosses, co-workers, know-it-all parakeets, talking snowmen, the list goes on.

And though this is technically an advice book, it is not the typical stuffy and boring sort because, unlike most advice books, this one is chock-full of: suspense, danger, adventure, mystery, simple yet delicious recipes for squash, and, of course, paper, since that's what books are generally chock-full of.

I should also inform you that, in addition to the above-mentioned elements, you will also encounter within the pages of this book words that are not present in any dictionary but, by all rights, should be.

Dictionaries, in my experience, are full of words that most people will never, ever use. Words like *tripanosomiasis*, *benzaldehyde*, and *kloof*. At the same time, the snobbish dictionary conglomerates refuse to include words that people commonly use on a daily basis.

Words such as *nother*, as in "That's a whole nother story."

Or *boughten*, as in "I haven't boughten a dictionary in years."

And may I say that I am most pleased you have boughten this book and I hope you enjoy reading it as much as I've enjoyed plagiarizing it from freeway overpass graffiti.

And just think, if you hadn't boughten this book, you would never have discovered the invaluable advice contained herein. And you would never have been able to share in the harrowing adventures and narrow escapes of Mr. Ethan Cheeseman and his three children, who, you will soon find, are quite possibly the most friendless and, conversely, the least friendful children in the entire United States.

CHAPTER 1

If you're anything like me, and most of you are by virtue of cell structure, you'll agree that there's nothing quite so sad as a child with no friends.

The children of Mr. Ethan Cheeseman found themselves in a near-constant state of friendlessness through absolutely no fault of their own. By all accounts the three youngsters were smart, pleasant, witty, attractive, polite, and relatively odor free. All traits that generally result in one having plenty of friends.

Their state of perennial friendlessness could be attributed solely to the fact that they were never in one place long enough to form any lasting relationships. You see, Ethan Cheeseman was a scientist and inventor by trade and, when he moved closer to perfecting a device so incredible, a device that could be used for either immense good or unspeakable evil, he found that suddenly everyone—from corporate criminals to top secret government agencies to international superspies—desired to get their hands on his brilliant new creation.

Ethan realized that this remarkable device would only ever be safe in his own hands. And so, one night he made a decision. He would disassemble the partially completed machine, load it into the family station wagon along with his three sleepy children, and disappear. And he would remain in a state of disappearedness until this device, known simply as the LVR, could be completed, perfected, and used to reclaim the life of Olivia, his beautiful wife and mother of his three smart, polite, and relatively odor-free children.

That was nearly two years ago, and since then Mr. Cheeseman and his children have been on the run, scarcely keeping one step ahead of these corporate villains, foreign intelligence operatives, and members of government agencies so secretive that no one, not even those who work for them, knows their names.

Of course there is much more to be told about all that, but it will have to wait because, at this very moment, Mr. Cheeseman is busy waking his children so he can once again hurry them into the family station wagon, along with all of their earthly possessions, and move them to yet another town, far away from those who have designs on his wonderfully useful yet incomplete invention.

"Let's go now," said Mr. Cheeseman, bursting into the room where his two boys slept peacefully and completely unaware. "We must be out of here in less than an hour."

"It's three in the morning," groaned fourteen-year-old Barton, the eldest of Mr. Cheeseman's three bright children. "Can't we sleep a little longer? I was having this great dream about pitching a no-hitter in the World Series."

"Big deal," came a voice from across the room. "You always have that dream." The voice belonged to Barton's eight-year-old brother, Crandall, who had a habit of waking up in a very grumpy state regardless of the time.

"Yes, but the dream is always ruined when I suddenly realize that I'm not wearing pants," said Barton. "This is the first time I remembered to wear pants and I'm not even allowed to enjoy it. It's not every day you get to pitch a no-hitter in the World Series with your pants on."

Mr. Cheeseman flipped on the light, an action that resulted in even more groaning.

"One day you will pitch a no-hitter in the World Series for real," said Mr. Cheeseman, always supportive of his children's ambitions. "But not if we don't get out of here ahead of the coats."

Coats was the term Mr. Cheeseman used to refer to all spies, corporate hoodlums, and members of hypersecret government agencies that would make the CIA seem very much like a church choir.

"Why won't they leave us alone?" asked Crandall.

Actually, the question was posed by Crandall's sock puppet, which Crandall had named Steve and was never without.

It was a gift from his mother, and Crandall and Steve the sock puppet were virtually inseparable. Ever since she passed away from a mysterious illness, practically no one had seen Crandall's left forearm, not even Crandall himself. It was constantly covered by the snarky sock puppet,

6

which, over the years, had become marbled with various unidentifiable stains and was missing its left eye.

This is worth mentioning because, after all, when you think about it, a sock puppet is really nothing more than a sock with a couple of plastic eyeballs glued on. This meant that Steve the sock puppet was only one eyeball away from being a mere sock, a condition that may have contributed to his overall snarkiness.

Steve never missed an opportunity to comment on anything and everything in his annoyingly squeaky voice, which sounded not unlike a dolphin with laryngitis, if you can imagine such horrible squeaking.

"I think we should stay and fight them instead of running all the time," said Steve, with an unintentional wink.

"We've been over this a hundred times, Steve," said Mr. Cheeseman, using all the patience he could muster. "Now boys, please hurry. Both of you."

Steve the sock puppet cleared his throat.

"Sorry," said Mr. Cheeseman. "I mean all three of you."

The boys dragged themselves from their beds with the most sorrowful sounds imaginable. Crandall reached up to the top of the bedpost where a large wad of pink, dust-covered goo rested. He tugged at the puttylike substance but it absolutely refused to budge.

"My gum won't come off," he whined. "It's stuck."

"Borrow your sister's hair dryer," said Mr. Cheeseman, who seemed to have an answer for just about everything. "Scientifically speaking, the heat will increase the speed of the atomic particles that make up the gum and should loosen it up nicely. Now let's move it. And Barton?"

"Yes, Dad?"

"Don't forget your pants."

In the bathroom down the hall, the boys' sister, Saffron, was already up, standing before the mirror and combing her long, wavy, auburn hair.

In these situations, Mr. Cheeseman always woke Saffron first, giving her a little extra time with her hair, which she washed each morning with her specially formulated wheat germ, honey, strawberry, coconut, apple pectin shampoo with pineapple and Canadian bacon.

After a lengthy lathering, her hair would be treated with cream rinse, followed by a conditioner, special split-end repair, and four hundred strokes from a brush made of imported porcupine quills.

Her attention to her hair should in no way be taken to mean that she was what is known as a girlie-girl. In fact, she was quite adept at very non-girlie-girl things such as running, jumping, archery, and putting her little brother into a headlock whenever it became necessary to do so. It should also be noted that her extensive hair-care regimen was carried out not of vanity but out of fondness for her mother, Olivia. Young Saffron was, at twelve years old, the spitting image of her late mother, who had the most beautiful auburn hair that has ever grown on any head, human or otherwise.

When Saffron looked into the mirror, she felt as though she were looking at the soft and pretty face of her mother, in a way. This gave Saffron comfort and hope that she might one day see her mother alive again.

Of course there would be absolutely no chance of that ever happening if the LVR, which incidentally stands for Luminal Velocity Regulator, were to fall into the wrong hands.

As Saffron continued to groom her shimmery locks, Pinky, the family dog, trotted into the bathroom, put her front paws up onto the toilet seat, leaned in as far as she could, and began lapping at the water. This was something Pinky did every day, except for two weeks in December when she chose instead to drink from the Christmas tree stand. Other than that, drinking from the toilet was a daily routine for the amiable fox terrier.

This, you would think, should be a practice that most dog owners would attempt to discourage. But if not for their dog's peculiar habit, Mr. Cheeseman and his three children would certainly have been nabbed by any one of their many pursuers. Simply put, Pinky's bad behavior had, on numerous occasions, saved their lives.

Allow me a moment of your time to explain.

By the time Olivia had finally succumbed to her mysterious illness, she had been taking many, many different medications. So many that the various bottles barely fit into the medicine chest above the sink in the bathroom.

When Ethan made the decision to go into hiding with his family so he could safely complete work on the LVR, he packed up all of their belongings. A notorious neat freak, he cleaned the house from top to bottom. This included getting rid of his late wife's many bottles of medicine.

Which brings us back to Pinky, the family dog.

Now, everyone knows you cannot dispose of prescription medication simply by throwing it into the trash. It could be discovered by young children who might mistake the brightly colored pills for candy. Thus, as I'm sure you already know, the medicine must always be flushed.

And so, one early, gray morning in February, as his children slept, Mr. Cheeseman stood at the medicine chest dumping bottle after bottle of pills into the toilet. The tablets plopped into the water like handfuls of pebbles on a calm, clear lake, albeit a very small lake, contained entirely within a porcelain bowl. Mixed in with the falling pills was a generous helping of Mr. Cheeseman's tears. And as he stood there, weeping and turning the toilet water a murky grayish purple with the dissolving pills, the phone rang.

Because Mr. Cheeseman was expecting a very important call from the police, he stopped what he was doing and walked to the living room to find the phone resting in its cradle. He wiped his eyes, gave his nose a few good sniffs, and answered the phone. He was immediately annoyed to find that the person at the other end of the line was not the important phone call he had been expecting. In fact, it was someone with whom he had no desire to speak whatsoever.

This undesirable person was calling, he said, to see if Mr. Cheeseman was happy with his current long-distance telephone service and, if not, would he be willing to switch to another service that might save him up to fifty dollars a month.

When Mr. Cheeseman returned to the bathroom, he was horrified to see Pinky engaged in her early morning quench, lapping at the purplish gray water in the toilet.

"Pinky! No!" Mr. Cheeseman shouted.

But it was too late.

In the few seconds he had been gone, the dog had ingested, along with several hundred tears, the contents of numerous and various pills, liquefied and joined together in a sort of medicinal stew.

When Pinky heard Mr. Cheeseman holler, she spun around with a crazed look in her eyes, which seemed to move completely independent of each other. She growled something in what sounded like an ancient Viking dialect, then promptly completed a dozen spins in a counterclockwise direction as Mr. Cheeseman watched helplessly.

"Pinky, are you okay? Come here, girl," he said, squatting down so he could look directly into the dog's spasmodic eyes.

As Ethan leaned closer to Pinky, speaking in soothing tones, she spun one last time and then suddenly bolted from the room between the stunned scientist's legs.

From the bathroom, Pinky ran into the living room. That is not to say that she ran from the bathroom to the living room, but that she actually ran *into* the living room.

Into the wall, knocking off several photos and leaving a fairly noticeable fox terrier–sized dent.

She then promptly turned around and ran headlong into the opposite wall, creating much the same effect. She continued this frenetic exercise for a good five minutes, leaving no wall unscathed until, finally, the dog completed a dozen or more spins and collapsed onto the floor, looking very much like a drunken pirate. That is, if dogs could be pirates.

For days, Pinky lay in a coma and the children kept an around-the-clock vigil at her bedside, hoping and praying that she would one day come back to them. Then, on the very day they were to leave behind the only life they had ever known, Pinky suddenly stood up, yawned, and gave herself a shake, causing every last bit of her hair to fall out, leaving her completely bald and appropriately pink while leaving the carpet a hairy mess.

And though she would remain completely hairless, she seemed otherwise entirely back to normal, or as normal as a dog that drinks from the toilet can be.

But as the weeks and months went by and Mr. Cheeseman and his three children moved from one town to the next, always keeping one step ahead of the coats, it soon became apparent that there was something very different about Pinky.

Pinky, it seemed, had somehow developed psychic abilities, which enabled her to sense danger and warn of disaster long before it happened.

Her knack for identifying perilous situations and

individuals with evil intent was uncanny. It was quite impossible to watch a whodunit on television with Pinky in the room because the minute the bad guy appeared on the screen Pinky would give it away by narrowing her eyes and growling through clenched teeth.

Her unique abilities had saved Mr. Cheeseman and his children from many a close call, including this very night when she burst into Mr. Cheeseman's room, jumped up onto the bed, and emitted a low growl that had become her trademark portent of doom.

"What is it, Pinky?" Mr. Cheeseman muttered.

"Grrrr," Pinky answered.

"Are you sure?"

"Grrrrrrrr!"

"Okay, okay."

Once the children were up and dressed and had packed their suitcases, Mr. Cheeseman ordered them to gather in the boys' room and wait there while he prepared the car for their escape.

"It's not fair," said Saffron as she threw a paperback book across the boys' bedroom, bouncing it off the closet door. This may seem like an odd thing to throw considering that books are not terribly aerodynamic. She threw the book because it was the only thing she could find to throw. Just about everything else—toys, clothing, school supplies, Barton's baseball equipment, Saffron's archery equipment, and Crandall's collection of dirt clods shaped like famous people—had all been packed up and loaded into the family station wagon.

"I don't want to move again," Saffron continued, searching in vain for something else to throw. The only thing she could find was Crandall's giant blob of pink, flavorless bubble gum still firmly affixed to his bedpost. Much stronger than her little brother, she yanked it from its perch and flung it across the room, where it stuck firmly to the wall about six feet above floor level.

"Hey, that's my gum," Crandall protested while running across the room, dragging his suitcase behind him, as the blob had landed well above his natural reach.

"Keep it down, you guys," said Barton. "Dad's got enough to worry about without listening to you fighting."

"How's he going to hear us?" asked Saffron. "He's out in the garage loading up that stupid machine."

"You shouldn't say *stupid*," said Crandall as he stood on the suitcase and, with his non-sock-puppet hand, peeled the bubble gum from the wall and then popped it into his mouth. "*Stupid* is a bad word."

"Stupid is putting something in your mouth that has been stuck to a wall," Saffron snapped back. For a moment, no one said anything. Then Saffron sat down on the bed and dropped her face into her hands.

"I'm sorry," she said. "I know why we have to move. I'm just tired, that's all."

"We're all tired of moving," said Barton.

"I liked this house," said Crandall sadly as he sat beside

his older sister. "I liked the way the driveway smelled when it rained."

"I liked the plum tree out back," said Saffron.

"I liked the fuzzy carpet," said Steve.

"Don't worry," said Barton. "I'm sure the next house will have lots of nice things about it as well."

"You never know," said Saffron. "Remember the light blue house with the leaky roof and the people next door who yelled all the time? There was nothing good about that house."

"Yeah," said Crandall. "And what about that old farm-house that got so cold at night and made those creepy noises?"

"At least we were only there for six weeks," Barton reminded him.

The bedroom door popped open and Mr. Cheeseman walked in with Pinky on his heels. "Okay, gang. Let's move out."

Saffron gave her reflection in the bedroom window one last glance and decided her hair looked good enough for the purposes of escaping under cover of darkness. Her brothers, on the other hand, seemed to have no interest whatsoever in how their hair looked.

Barton at least had the decency to put on a baseball cap so his sheeply mass of black curls only stuck out from the sides and back. They matched in color, if not thickness, his recently arrived teenage mustache, of which Barton was very proud even though it was quite patchy and uneven and, from a distance, could be mistaken for crumbs of burned toast.

When it came to grooming, Crandall was another matter altogether. His short blond hair shot out in all directions and his big, round, spiky head reminded Saffron of something in a comic book when one character is hit in the head by another. Inside the jagged bubble, you might see the words *Kapow*, *Blammo*, or *Zoinks*.

To make matters worse, Crandall's bald spot had not yet fully grown back. Less than a week before, Crandall had fallen asleep while chewing a wad of bubble gum roughly the size of a billiard ball, something his father had warned him against repeatedly. The following morning, Crandall awoke with Steve the sock puppet firmly stuck to his head, bonded tightly by the hardened pink goo, which had fallen from the boy's mouth as he slept.

Following a two-hour operation involving peanut butter, scissors, and crying, Steve the sock puppet and Crandall the crying boy were no longer joined at the head, but each sported a bald spot roughly the size and shape of a silver-dollar pancake. Now, nearly a week later, Crandall's bald spot had partially grown back, though Steve, being a mere sock puppet, would have no such luck.

"Barton?" said Mr. Cheeseman. "What about your ear-muffs?"

"Dad, I'm fine."

"I'd appreciate it if you'd put them on just 'til we get rolling. I'd hate to have you fall over and break your arm on the way to the car."

"I've been cured of that, Dad, really."

Though interested in sports and very athletic, Barton often fell over due to an inner ear imbalance he had had since birth. To give you an idea as to how serious a malady this was, on one occasion he fell down a flight of stairs. It was an escalator going up and he kept falling for two hours until, finally, the mall closed for the night.

This is where having a brilliant scientist and inventor for a father can come in quite handy. Mr. Cheeseman developed a special set of earmuffs that send out inaudible sound waves to help maintain perfect inner ear balance.

Barton sighed and pulled the earmuffs from his pocket and put them on.

"Thanks. I appreciate that," said Mr. Cheeseman. "Now, how about the rest of you? Are you sure you've got everything?"

"I've got everything," said Crandall.

"Me too," said Steve the sock puppet.

"Oh no," said Saffron. "I think I forgot my hairbrush."

"Who cares about your stupid hairbrush?" said Steve, to which Saffron replied by soundly bonking him on his patchy, one-eyed sock puppet head.

"Blammo!"

A BIT OF ADVICE FOR INVENTORS

What separates us humans from the animals, besides indoor plumbing, the right to vote, and wrinkle-free slacks, is our capacity to invent things. Things like . . . wrinkle-free slacks.

Even monkeys, as smart as they might be, have never invented anything. It remains a cold hard fact that even the monkey wrench was invented not by a monkey but by a human. In addition, the dogsled, the bear hug, the crow's nest, the fish-eye lens, and the catamaran were all invented by humans, not animals. Nothing has ever been invented by an animal, though there are those who, to this day, will argue that horseplay was indeed invented by horses.

Regardless, the point is that human beings are, by far, the planet's most prolific inventors. Perhaps the greatest of these inventors was Thomas Alva Edison, who invented, among other things, the name Alva. To give you an idea as to the genius of Edison you should know that at the time of his death he held over twelve hundred patents, which was a lot of weight for a person his age to be holding and is most likely what killed him.

The patent is the one and only way an inventor can protect himself or herself from those who might wish to steal an idea. Without the benefit of a patent, it is entirely possible that an inventor could be denied any and all credit for a brilliant invention.

The wheel, for example, was one of the first inventions of early man that resulted in making him even earlier, provided he did not attempt to travel during rush hour.

The wheel is arguably the greatest innovation of all time, though the name of its inventor remains a mystery because in those days there were no patents. There were no patents because there were no lawyers. That is, until after the wheel was invented and ran over some people. Then there were lawyers everywhere.

And so my advice to any and all would-be inventors is to make sure you patent and protect your ideas if you wish to receive the proper credit. And, as in the case of Mr. Ethan Cheeseman, I would advise you to be extremely careful that you do not invent something so fantastically wonderful and useful that you become the target of corporate villains, international super-spies, and government agencies so secret that their names are not known.

CHAPTER 2

Mr. Cheeseman and his three smart, witty, attractive, polite, and relatively odor-free children were packed up and ready to move away, once again, to their new home, which they all hoped would have a sound roof and a pleasant-smelling driveway.

"Okay, this is it," said Mr. Cheeseman. He flipped off the light in the boys' room, and when he did he saw something through the window that caused his eyes to narrow.

"What is it, Dad?" asked Barton. "What's wrong?"

"They're here," said Mr. Cheeseman, his gaze fixed on a gray sedan parked out front, beneath the dull glow of a streetlight. "They're already here."

"Grrrrr," said Pinky.

"What do we do now?" asked Saffron. In the two years they'd been on the run, this was the first time they hadn't gotten away before the coats arrived.

"I can't promise it'll work," said Mr. Cheeseman, nervously biting his lower lip. "But I've got an idea."

Mr. Cheeseman led the children through the darkened

house and into the garage, where the rusted white station wagon was loaded to the ceiling with all it could hold in the way of toys, clothing, dirt clods shaped like celebrities, and the LVR, disassembled into several large pieces and covered with a blue tarp.

As always, the car had been backed into the garage, its nose facing the door to help hasten a last-minute escape.

"Even if we do get past them," said Barton, "won't they just follow us?"

"I think they'll try," said Mr. Cheeseman. "But if all goes according to plan, they won't get very far."

"Why not?" asked Barton.

"A little invention I like to call the Inertia Ray," said Mr. Cheeseman as he helped a very sleepy Crandall into the backseat.

"What's an Inertia Ray?" wondered Saffron.

"I came up with the idea while working on the LVR, which operates on the principle that the speed of light can be manipulated to alter the speed of objects in its path," Mr. Cheeseman explained. "Scientifically speaking, people who are struck by a beam of light traveling at several times the speed of light will be temporarily rendered motionless."

"But how can light travel faster than the speed of light?" asked Barton. "That's impossible."

"Not necessarily," said Saffron, not about to miss an opportunity to show off her oversized brain. "Light could be made to travel faster than the speed of light the same way a tortoise could be made to travel faster than the speed of a tortoise. By boarding a fast-moving train or an airplane."

"Exactly," said Mr. Cheeseman. "The Inertia Ray is to light as that jet airplane is to the tortoise."

"I understand that," said Saffron. "But how will it help us now?"

"Well, that's obvious," said Barton. "Tell her, Dad."

"It's simple, really," said Mr. Cheeseman. "Last night, I hooked up the Inertia Ray to the high beams of the station wagon. Let's hope I did it correctly because right now it's our only hope of getting out of here."

With that, Mr. Cheeseman fired up the engine. He took a deep breath and narrowed his eyes, then clicked the automatic garage door opener. Slowly, the door peeled away to reveal the gray car parked directly across the street.

"Keep your fingers crossed," said Mr. Cheeseman. "Here we go."

He hit the gas and the station wagon bolted from the garage. As the car neared the end of the driveway, Mr. Cheeseman hit the high beams, aiming them directly at the gray car. As Mr. Cheeseman turned left and drove past the car, the children looked out to see a man dressed in a gray suit behind the wheel, completely frozen in time, like a wax figure holding a cell phone, his mouth open in mid-sentence. In the passenger seat was another man dressed in gray, taking a bite of a sandwich, and he was likewise frozen in time.

"It worked!" said Barton.

"It sure did," said Mr. Cheeseman, perfectly pleased with his latest invention. "It's only a temporary effect but it should give us a good ten minutes or so before they snap out of it."

Just then, with a squealing of tires, a little brown car turned from a side street and moved in directly behind them.

"Dad," said Barton.

"I see them," said Mr. Cheeseman.

"What do we do?" asked Saffron.

"What do we do?" Mr. Cheeseman repeated. "We hold on!"

With that, Mr. Cheeseman hit the gas, temporarily pulling away from the brown car. But the station wagon was a slow-moving car to begin with. Load it down with four people, a disassembled, nonworking time machine, several boxes of toys, books, clothing, and dirt clods and you'd be lucky to outrun a three-wheeled shopping cart.

Within seconds the little brown car regained its ground and pulled up directly behind them.

"Prepare for evasive maneuvers," Mr. Cheeseman shouted to his children over his shoulder.

Their heads snapped to the left as Mr. Cheeseman cranked the wheel hard to the right, causing the tires to chirp loudly as the station wagon flew down a side street. The brown car made the same turn, but much more cautiously, thus giving the station wagon a good fifty-foot head start.

"Okay, everybody," Mr. Cheeseman warned. "Hold on tight, 'cause here we go!"

As the brown car began to close the gap, Mr. Cheeseman stomped on the brake pedal while cranking the wheel to the left as far as it would go, causing the station wagon to fly into a violent spin, at one point rolling up onto two wheels.

When it finally came to rest back on all of its wheels, the station wagon was facing in the opposite direction, with the brown car speeding directly toward it.

"Dad, look out!" Barton shouted as he cowered behind the dashboard.

The driver of the brown car hit the brakes but it slowed only slightly as it skidded toward a head-on collision with the station wagon. Barton dug his fingernails into the dashboard. Saffron hid her face in her hands. Crandall and Steve hugged each other tightly, preparing for the worst.

With less than two seconds to impact, Mr. Cheeseman reached up and hit the high-beam switch, sending a stream of light traveling at several times the speed of light directly at the brown car. Instantly the car froze.

Mr. Cheeseman threw the station wagon into reverse and backed up a few feet before putting it in drive and screaming off down the street, leaving their pursuers in suspended animation.

Saffron uncovered her eyes. Crandall and Steve did not stop hugging each other. Barton pulled his fingernails from the dashboard.

Though he hid it well, Barton was secretly embarrassed by how he had reacted so cowardly in the face of danger. Silently he vowed that the next time he found himself in similar circumstances, he would respond bravely like his father, like a true man of action. "That was close," he gasped, feeling as though he might pass out.

"It sure was," said Mr. Cheeseman. "I must remember for future reference to install the Inertia Ray on the taillights as well."

"Dad?" Crandall asked. "Is everything going to be okay?"

"I hope so," said Mr. Cheeseman. "But only time will tell."

SOME TIMELY ADVICE ON TIME TRAVEL

If there's one thing we can all agree on, it's what time it is. We humans have been fighting for centuries over things like which god and/or gods to worship, or who owns which chunk of land, or who shot a fellow named Archduke Ferdinand. Never once, however, has there been a major war or serious skirmish over the correct time. We all seem to agree that an hour is made up of sixty minutes, a minute is composed of sixty seconds, and a second is equal to one Mississippi. The fact that we agree on this is significant because it means that all those wars about other things always begin exactly on schedule.

But what would happen if we could suddenly change the time? I'm not talking about daylight saving or about people who intentionally set their watches five minutes fast so they will never be late but will be required to do math anytime someone asks them for the correct time.

"Excuse me, do you have the time?" people say to them.

"Well, let's see," they answer. "My watch says 3:03 so I'll have to borrow from the zero. Yes, it's 2:98."

What I'm talking about here is much bigger than reset-ting your watch. I'm talking about changing the very time that encircles you, altering the time in which you exist.

What if a device could transport us to any time in his-tory, or prehistory for that matter? How could we change the past to improve the present and secure the future for all humankind? For years, scientists have hypothesized that one day time travel will be a reality, though never with more than two carry-on bags.

The question remains, however, as to whether this is a good thing. What effect will changing the past have on the present and the future? I would advise anyone traveling across the time/space continuum to respect the past because, without it, the present might very well cease to exist.

A wise man once said, "Those who forget the past are condemned to repeat it," and that would be a terri-ble thing because, as a wise man once said, "Those who forget the past are condemned to repeat it."

CHAPTER 3

Mr. Cheeseman had been driving for three hours when finally night began to move aside and the new day inched slowly above the distant hills.

"Okay, gang," said Mr. Cheeseman, checking his rearview mirror and happy to find that it remained completely free of pursuers. "Looks like we made it. Pinky hasn't growled in over an hour, so at least for the time being, it appears as though we're out of danger."

"Can we do the names now?" Crandall said with a yawn.

The only fun part about being on the run from various pursuers, all falling over themselves to get their hands on the LVR, was that each time Mr. Cheeseman and his family moved, he required the children to completely change their identities. This was done for their own safety. And the best part was that they were each allowed to choose their own names, both first and last, with absolutely no interference from their father, who felt that a child's creativity should never be harnessed.

"Sure," said Mr. Cheeseman. "If you're ready."

"I'm ready," said Crandall. "I've already got my new name all picked out. From now on, you can call me . . ."

Crandall paused for dramatic effect as he always did, chewing on his giant wad of flavorless bubble gum.

". . . Gerard LaFontaine."

Mr. Cheeseman rubbed his chin and nodded his head slowly, also for dramatic effect.

"I like it," he said. "Good work, Gerard."

"Thanks," said Gerard, who in the past had gone by such names as Ernesto Diablo, Johnny Cigar, Carlton J. Moneypants, and, most recently, Crandall Moriarty.

"Hmm, I don't know. You don't really look like a Gerard," said Saffron, who in the past had given herself such names as Lucretia Dee, Paprika Jones, Salmonella Sneezeguard, and, most recently, Saffron Ponderosa.

"I kind of like it," said Barton. "It sounds . . . sophisticated."

"That's what I mean," said Saffron with a flip of her auburn hair. "Doesn't really suit him at all."

"I am so phosisticrated," said the newly named Gerard. "Anyway, it's probably better than your new name, Saffron."

"I will thank you," replied Saffron, "to address me by my proper name, which, from this point forward, will be Magenta-Jean Jurgenson."

Gerard's first inclination was to make fun of his sister's new name, but he had to admit that Magenta-Jean Jurgenson had a pretty good ring to it, and so he decided to simply keep his mouth shut.

Steve the sock puppet, on the other hand (the left hand, to be precise), showed no such restraint and blurted out, "That's the dumbest name I've ever heard."

Saffron, or I should say Magenta-Jean, reached out and flicked Steve the sock puppet with her middle finger.

"Zoinks!"

"Well, I like it very much," said Mr. Cheeseman. "It is a bit of a mouthful, however."

"You can call me Maggie for short," said Magenta-Jean. "Unless you're angry with me. Then you can say, 'Magenta-Jean Jurgenson, you get in here this instant!'"

"Come now," said Mr. Cheeseman, looking at his daughter in the rearview mirror. "When was the last time I got angry with you?"

"October sixteenth of last year," said Maggie, who had nothing short of an incredible memory. "About four forty in the afternoon."

"Well, I don't remember that at all," said Mr. Cheeseman. "Why was I angry with you?"

"If you don't remember, then I don't think I'll remind you," said Maggie.

"Point well made, Maggie," said Mr. Cheeseman. "Okay, Barton, you're next. Have you decided on a new name for yourself?"

"Yup," said Barton, who had previously answered to such names as Figaro Lowenstein, Antoine Razorback, Lucias Aloisius von Dignacious III, and, most recently, Barton Burton. "My new name will be Joe Smith."

Maggie and Gerard immediately broke into laughter,

assuming their older brother must be joking. When he himself failed to so much as crack a smile, they knew he must be serious.

"Joe Smith?" said Gerard. "That's not very posistiphated."

"I hate to say it," said Maggie, twirling a strand of reddish hair around her index finger, "but I kind of agree with Gerard. Joe Smith just seems kind of . . . boring."

"Well," said Mr. Cheeseman, "it is slightly less imaginative than we've come to expect from you."

"But Dad, you're jumping to conclusions before having all the evidence—something you've always told us not to do. Sure, the name Joe Smith might be kind of boring. Unless it looks like this."

He handed his father a piece of paper upon which he had written the name *Jough Psmythe*.

Mr. Cheeseman took his eyes off the road and rearview mirror long enough to glance at the piece of paper. He said nothing and simply broke into a smile that indicated "That's more like it."

"What is it?" clamored Gerard. "What does it say?"

Mr. Cheeseman handed the piece of paper back over his shoulder and, as Gerard reached for it, Maggie snatched it away.

"Jough Psmythe?" she said, wadding up the paper in disgust.

"What? You don't like it?" asked Jough, who could be very sensitive about such things.

"That's not it at all," said Maggie. "In fact, I have to admit it's perfect. I only wish I had come up with it first."

"That's ridiculous," said Steve the sock puppet. "Jough is a boy's name."

Back near the pale yellow house that Mr. Cheeseman and his children had most recently called home, the occupants of the gray car and the little brown car had shaken off the effects of the Inertia Ray and had returned to normal—only to find that the white station wagon had vanished.

Meanwhile, a third car, a long black sedan with equally black windows, pulled slowly into the driveway of the yellow house just as the gray car was driving away.

The doors opened and four men in dark suits and dark sunglasses hopped out of the car. Truth be told, this is only an expression: they did not actually hop out of the car, as this would not only increase one's chances of hitting one's head on the way out but also look very silly.

And trust me when I say that these were not men who were in the habit of doing anything to make themselves look silly.

As the serious-looking men stood before the pale yellow house, none of them gave even the slightest thought to the lovely smell of the freshly wet pavement of the driveway.

Instead, three of the men looked to the fourth as if awaiting instructions. The man they looked to was known only as Mr. 5.

The other three were known as Mr. 29, Mr. 88, and

Mr. 207. This should give you an idea as to just how important Mr. 5 was in the grand scheme of things.

Tall and slim, Mr. 5 had an exceedingly bony face and cheeks so hollow it looked as if they were sewn tightly together from the inside. His bald, sweaty head and his large reflective sunglasses gave him the look of a shiny, pale insect.

Without speaking, he nodded toward Mr. 88 and Mr. 207. The two men nodded back, apparently in complete agreement with what Mr. 5 had not said.

The two men then walked around the side of the house toward the backyard, leaving Mr. 5 and Mr. 29, a fellow of enormous size with giant rings on each finger of his right hand, standing in the driveway. Mr. 5 walked up the steps to the front porch and Mr. 29 followed dutifully.

When they reached the front door, Mr. 5 looked at his oversized compatriot and nodded as if what they were about to do they had done a thousand times before. Mr. 29 responded to the nod by removing a small but powerful set of bolt cutters from his pocket. He applied the bolt cutters to the door handle and, with one quick snap with his enormous hands, clipped off the entire doorknob, causing it to fall to the ground and bounce down the front stairs and roll into a flower bed, nearly crushing a ladybug named Doris.

Again Mr. 5 nodded toward Mr. 29, who simply responded by kicking in the front door to the house. He kicked with such force that the door actually said goodbye to its hinges and fell onto the living room floor.

"They're gone," said Mr. 29.

"I can see that, you idiot," hissed Mr. 5 as he grabbed the large man's necktie and pulled him close to his unnaturally bony face. "The question is, why are they gone?"

Mr. 5 released Mr. 29's necktie and wiped a bead of cold sweat from his clammy forehead. As he did, the sleeve of his left arm receded just far enough to reveal a series of letters and numbers tattooed on his wrist in dark black ink. The oddly cryptic tattoo read *3VAW1X319*.

Just then, Mr. 88 and Mr. 207 burst in through the back door.

"Looks like they're gone," said Mr. 207.

"Brilliant deduction," said Mr. 5. "Did your mother drop you on your head? And what is that in your hand?"

"It's a plum," replied Mr. 207, biting into the bright purple fruit. "There's a tree out back. Very nice flavor."

"Get rid of it! This is not snack time!"

Mr. 207 sheepishly tossed the partially eaten plum to the floor.

"We're here for one reason and one reason only," said Mr. 5, pacing around the room. "Do you understand me?"

The three men all nodded agreeably.

"This is the seventh time now. The seventh time that we have responded to information as to their whereabouts, and the seventh time we've arrived too late. Somebody must be tipping them off. Someone inside the company."

Mr. 5 looked suspiciously at the three men standing before him.

"Well . . . certainly you don't think it was one of us," said Mr. 88.

"It's possible, isn't it?" said Mr. 5 as he squatted down to inspect a doggie chew toy left behind in the panic. "Who do you think is tipping them off? The family dog?"

"No sir," said Mr. 88 with an incredulous chuckle.

"Of course not! But when I find out who is responsible, that person will wish he had never been born. That I promise you."

Mr. 5 reached into his breast pocket and pulled out a very small cell phone, about the size of a matchbook. He put the phone to his mouth and spoke a single word.

"Headquarters."

He waited for a moment, then a woman's voice came through the earpiece.

"Headquarters. Go ahead, Mr. 5."

"Yes," said Mr. 5. "I need to speak to Mr. 1 immediately."

"I'm sorry, but Mr. 1 is unavailable at this moment. May I take a message?"

"No, you may not." Mr. 5 scowled. "Let me speak to Mr. 2."

"Mr. 2 is in a meeting, but I'd be happy to—"

"Very well," said Mr. 5, quickly losing his patience. "Let me speak to—"

"I'm afraid Mr. 3 is also unavailable. Would you like me to put you through to Ms. 4?"

Just the mention of Ms. 4's name made Mr. 5's face look as though it hurt very badly.

"Fine," he huffed. "I will speak to Ms. 4."

"One moment please," said the voice at the other end.

Mr. 5 covered the mouthpiece of the tiny phone with his thumb, then spun around to face the others. "We have failed for the last time, gentlemen. Next time, we will find them and we will crush them."

This bit of information seemed to pique Mr. 88's interest.

"How?" he asked.

"How what?" said Mr. 5, his thumb still pressed over the mouthpiece.

"How will we crush them? Will we use one of those giant machines at the junkyard that they use to crush old cars? I think that would work pretty well."

"Or how about a steam roller?" Mr. 207 offered. "That would crush 'em real good, too."

"A steam roller?" scoffed Mr. 88. "That's for squishing, not crushing."

"Aren't they the same thing?" asked Mr. 207. "Squishing and crushing?"

"Hardly," said Mr. 88. "Take a tube of toothpaste, for instance. You don't crush it. You squish it from the bottom."

"I usually squeeze mine from the middle," said the normally silent Mr. 29. "My wife hates that."

"Would you shut up, all of you!" barked Mr. 5. "What does toothpaste have to do with anything?"

"Nothing," admitted Mr. 88. "I was only trying to figure out what might be the best method of crushing Mr. Cheeseman and his family."

"It was only a figure of speech, you idiot," said Mr. 5.

"Oh," said Mr. 88 with a sudden look of disappointment. "So then . . . no actual crushing?"

"No. I meant only that we will find them and destroy them. Ruin them. Devastate them to the point that they will wish they had never dared to defy us in the first place."

"I see," said Mr. 88 as he considered this for a moment. "How about squishing?"

On a small tropical island, somewhere in the southern hemisphere, there stood a large factory nearly hidden from view by the dense jungle foliage. On a hill above that factory was a large office building, and in that building was an office belonging to a small, thin-lipped woman with long red fingernails named Ms. 4. (That is not to say her long red fingernails were named Ms. 4 but that the woman herself was named that. As of this writing, the woman had not named her fingernails.)

The phone on her desk emitted a low beep, followed by the sound of a young man's voice saying, "Ms. 4? Mr. 6 is on line 5. I'm sorry. Correction, Mr. 5 is on line 6."

The thin-lipped woman with the nameless red fingernails rearranged her face to look slightly annoyed, then reached out and picked up the phone on her desk.

"Hello, Mr. 5. What is the current status? Have you secured the LVR?"

"Someone must have tipped them off. We . . . lost them. Again," said Mr. 5, swallowing his pride.

"I would advise you, Mr. 5, not to fail again," said Ms. 4, looking out her window at the bustling factory below. "If you wish to keep your current position with the company."

"I believe I have already demonstrated that I will do whatever it takes to get the LVR. And I will get it. Or I will die trying," said Mr. 5, wiping his cold, moist, boney forehead with his tattooed left wrist.

"Yes. Yes, you will," said Ms. 4 through her thin lips.

SOME MUCH NEEDED ADVICE ON TATTOOS

There was a time when, if you encountered someone with a tattoo, you could pretty much assume he was either a sailor or had, at one time or another, been in prison. There was something, it seemed, about men being cooped up together that made them want to draw on themselves.

But lately, it's become more and more difficult to distinguish sailors and ex-convicts from regular folks, as everyone these days is getting a tattoo.

People who get tattoos are likely to say it is a great way to express their individuality. But before you decide to express your individuality by doing what everyone else is doing, be forewarned that tattoos are permanent.

What then if you happen to choose a tattoo that seems like a good idea at the time but one day outlives its usefulness?

For instance, I am acquainted with a young woman named Lois who was so enamored of her fiancé, Jack, that she thought it might be nice to surprise him by having the words *I love Jack* tattooed in bright red ink on her right shoulder blade.

Two days later, Jack surprised Lois by marrying someone else. And so, because tattoos are permanent, she was forced to return to the tattoo parlor and have the words *I love Jack* altered to read *I love flapjacks*.

That was some time ago. Since then Lois has gotten over Jack and is currently back on the dating scene, though she finds that all of her suitors end up taking her to dinner at the local pancake house.

This goes to show you that the only place you should ever have anyone's name written in indelible ink is on the waistband of your underwear. And then it should be your own name, as having someone else's name on your underwear would be both odd and highly inappropriate.

The point is that tattoos are permanent. Underwear is not.

Still, it seems that these days tattoos are outselling underwear two to one. As popular as they might be, I would advise against getting one at all costs. Because, as with my pancake-loving friend Lois, or with our sweaty, hollow-cheeked non-friend Mr. 5, there will come a day when you will most assuredly regret having it. This I absolutely guarantee or my name isn't . . . wait a minute. This is not my underwear.

CHAPTER 4

The hot afternoon sun seemed to melt the horizon like a gooey grilled cheese sandwich as the white station wagon rumbled down the two-lane highway.

Mr. Cheeseman and his family had been driving for nearly seven hours now, and in that time they had driven past several hundred gas stations, several thousand telephone poles, the world's largest hat, the world's smallest chicken, the Table Tennis Hall of Fame, eighty-seven truck stops, Cleveland, and, just a moment ago, the National Center for Unsolicited Advice.

I could clearly see them from the window of my palatial, well-appointed office as they rumbled down the narrow highway, flanked on either side by grassy fields, which were home to hundreds of happily grazing black and white cows.

For some reason known only to himself, eight-year-old Gerard LaFontaine removed the oversized wad of bubble gum from his mouth, stuck his head out the window, circled his hands around his mouth, and yelled, "Mooooo."

The cows, for the most part, ignored young Gerard, though one of the least intelligent of the herd did turn toward the car with a quizzical look that seemed to say "Dad? Is that you?"

Maggie turned to her younger brother and scoffed.

"Exactly what do you hope to accomplish by doing that?"

"Just making conversation," said Gerard.

"Well, you do look kind of like a cow, gnawing away on that giant wad of goop."

"It's not goop, it's bubble gum. And I have to chew it. It helps me think. I can't concentrate without it."

"That's ridiculous."

"Not really," said Mr. Cheeseman. "The results of a recent study showed a thirty-five percent increase in long- and short-term memory in subjects who chewed gum."

Gerard turned and looked at Maggie with enough smugness to make his point but not enough to get smacked across the chest.

"It also increases alertness," continued Mr. Cheeseman. "I'll take a piece if you can spare one, Gerard."

"Dad, if you're getting tired I could drive for a while," said Jough.

It was true that Mr. Cheeseman had taught his son to drive when Jough was just twelve years old. This may seem like a highly irresponsible thing for a parent to do, but in their current situation, his father weighed the risks and thought this would be a good skill for Jough to have. That way, if anything were to happen to him, Jough would be able to drive Gerard and Maggie to safety or to get help.

"It's okay, Jough. I'll let you know if I need your help. But thanks anyway."

"No problem," said Jough, barely hiding his disappointment.

"When are we gonna get there, anyway?" asked Gerard, handing his father a piece of gum.

"It's hard to say," said Mr. Cheeseman, "considering the fact that I'm not sure exactly where we're going."

"Maybe this time we could stay long enough that I could try out for summer league baseball," Jough said.

"That would be nice," said Mr. Cheeseman. "I'd like to see you use that screwball I taught you."

"I'd like to continue my archery lessons," said Maggie.

"I'd like to join the Cub Scouts," said Gerard.

"I'd like to get a paper route," said Steve.

"Grrrr," Pinky growled at the one-eyed sock puppet.

"I'm hoping we can do all those things," said Mr. Cheeseman. "Believe me, I'm just as tired of this lifestyle as you are. But you all know why we have to live this way, so let's just make the most of it and hope that it will all be over soon."

To look at the handsome, bespectacled driver of the heavily loaded white station wagon, you might never guess that Ethan Cheeseman was a veritable genius and one of the greatest inventors of this or any other century.

To be fair though, none of his inventions would ever have been realized if he hadn't been introduced to an equally brilliant scientist with long auburn hair named Olivia Lodbrok. (That is not to say her hair was named Olivia Lodrok but that the woman herself was named that. It had never occurred to the woman to name her hair.)

Olivia was a strikingly beautiful woman despite the fact that her large black-rimmed glasses covered nearly half her face. She had that rare face that could survive the addition of large black-rimmed glasses. In fact she was so beautiful that you could affix just about anything to her face—a giant squid, for instance, or a toy tractor, or a handlebar mustache—and she would still be every bit as attractive.

Olivia and Ethan fell madly in love, and the rest is history.

Truth be told, that's only an expression and the rest is not history. Not all of it, anyway. Quite a bit of it is, in fact, biology, as several years later Ethan and Olivia were married with three young children that you now know as Jough, Maggie, and Gerard. And though these were not their names at birth, I will refer to them by these names so as not to create unnecessary confusion.

Up until two years ago, Jough, Maggie, and Gerard were three of the happiest children there ever were. They attended school and had many friends. Jough, despite his problems with balance, was able to play baseball and touch football with the other neighborhood children with the help of his specially made earmuffs. He was popular and a good student, though he was secretly very annoyed by the fact that his younger sister had skipped ahead two entire grades and now sat directly in front of him in homeroom.

Maggie, like her mother, was smart as a whip and at the top of her class in just about every subject. She had received nothing but straight As since first grade, when they first begin handing out letter grades. Before that, in kindergarten, she had received straight happy faces. In addition to being a star pupil, she was also a natural athlete, excelling in cross-country running and archery.

Gerard was a child of incredible imagination who could carry on a conversation with just about any inanimate object, from a coat rack or a toaster oven to the salt and pepper shakers at home, which he had named Alvin and Berniece.

Together they lived in a small house with a large double garage. Even though they had only one car, a beat-up white station wagon, they needed the extra room so Mr. Cheeseman could work on his many inventions while Olivia worked on the scientific formulas and computer codes that would help make those inventions work.

One of those inventions was the LVR, a device originally designed as a means for mankind to travel from Earth to other planets in faraway galaxies. This has always been thought to be impossible because, for starters, the nearest star outside our own solar system is several light-years away.

For those who lack my extensive knowledge in the area of astronomy, allow me to explain the scientific meaning of the term "light-year." Without getting too technical I'll just say that a light-year is very much like a dog year with the exception that light, given the opportunity, will not drink from your toilet or growl at sock puppets. Simply put, if something is one light-year away, bring a snack because it's a long way to go.

Not the kind of people easily deterred by conventional wisdom or the laws of physics as we know them, Ethan and Olivia continued the development of the LVR. As they moved closer and closer to perfecting the technology, something strange began to happen. Even though Ethan and Olivia told no one about their latest project, not even their own children, people began showing up at their doorstep expressing interest in the partially completed machine.

It all started early one morning while the children were at school and Ethan was working away in the garage on the LVR, which, in its partly finished state, resembled a giant egg-shaped disco ball, covered with heat-resistant reflective mirrors and prisms. The interior could best be described as a combination of an airplane cockpit and a used motor home. Ethan hoped his light-bending device would be the first spacecraft to travel to other worlds, bringing a message of peace, brotherhood, and, quite possibly, disco.

As he stood at his workbench welding two pieces of tempered steel together, sparks danced off his welding mask. The doorbell rang but Ethan did not hear it over the sound of the welding torch. However, Olivia, working on the computer code in her office just off the kitchen, did.

Pinky followed Olivia to the door as she always did

when the doorbell rang, perhaps out of simple curiosity or in hope that the doorbell had been rung by a giant soup bone. Olivia opened the door to find not a giant soup bone but two men in gray suits standing on her doorstep. One was short with wide shoulders, a thin waist, and skinny legs, giving him the appearance of a kite with gray-rimmed glasses and gray hair.

The other man was tall with a wide bottom and a very narrow top. If he could somehow be convinced to put on a white suit and a red bow tie, he would bear a remarkable resemblance to a bowling pin.

The kite and the bowling pin worked for a top secret government agency in which all employees were known only by their initials, and the initials were always spelled out.

"Hello," said the kite-shaped man in a monotone voice. "My name is Agent Aitch Dee and this is Agent El Kyoo. We work for the United States government and we'd very much like to talk to you about your . . . current project." He used his fingers to put air quotes around "current project."

Pinky began sniffing at their gray shoes.

"Excuse me, but how do you know about our current project?" Olivia said, mimicking the man's finger quotes. "And how do I know you really work for the government?"

Pinky sniffed at their gray pant legs.

"He must smell my dog," said El Kyoo in a tone every bit as expressionless as his partner's. "I have a gray Pekinese at home." Both men pulled a gray leather billfold from the breast pocket of their gray suit jackets and opened them to reveal official government ID.

47

"Well, this says you work for the government but it doesn't say what department," said Olivia, carefully reading the documents.

"Our department doesn't have a name, ma'am," said El Kyoo. "I mean, it does, but we're not sure what it is. It's a very top secret organization."

"You mean like the CIA?"

The two agents looked at each other and their stony faces very nearly registered something close to amusement.

"Ma'am," began Aitch Dee, "the Cee Eye Ay doesn't even know we exist. But we do exist and for a very good reason. Now, if you don't mind, we'd like to ask you a few questions."

"Well, I don't think—," Olivia began.

"We would appreciate your cooperation," droned El Kyoo as Aitch Dee casually put his shoe in front of the door.

"Should the LVR fall into the wrong hands, it could prove disastrous. You owe it to your country to turn the machine over to us," said Aitch Dee.

"I'll decide what I owe and to whom, thank you. Anyway, my husband is the one you'd want to talk to and he just happens to be away at the moment."

"He's in the garage," said El Kyoo. "He's wearing blue coveralls, yellow work gloves, and a welding mask."

"And a wristwatch with a brown leather band," added Aitch Dee. "He had leftover birthday cake for breakfast this morning along with two glasses of chocolate milk. You see, Mrs. Cheeseman, there's nothing we don't know."

"Well, you certainly don't know when you've worn out your welcome," said Olivia, kicking Aitch Dee's shoe out from in front of the door. "Now if you'll excuse me."

Olivia, though a woman of small stature, was not someone to be intimidated easily.

"Mrs. Cheeseman," said Aitch Dee, before she could slam the door shut, "we can offer you protection."

"Protection? Protection from what?"

"Not from what," said El Kyoo. "From whom. There are people who will do anything to get their hands on that device of yours. Come work for us and we'll guarantee your safety."

"We can take care of ourselves," said Olivia as she quickly shut the door and locked it, then spied through the peephole, hoping the two gray-covered men would go away. She watched as they walked toward their gray car parked on the street across from the house. When they climbed inside the car, Olivia ran to the garage.

"The government?" Ethan said, lifting his welding mask to reveal his bemusement. "But how could they possibly know what we're working on?"

"I don't know, but they also know that you had leftover birthday cake and chocolate milk for breakfast," said Olivia.

"Uh . . . yes," said Ethan, who was known to have something of a sweet tooth. "I did have cake for breakfast. We were . . . all out of toast. As for the chocolate milk . . ."

"That's not important," said Olivia. "What is important is that they seem to know all about the LVR. Which means we have to be very careful to protect it."

This was Ethan and Olivia's first indication that they were on to something big. Something that could be used for either immense good or unspeakable evil, depending on who ended up with it. And everyone, it seemed, wanted to end up with the LVR.

For the next couple of days, everywhere Ethan and Olivia went they felt as though they were being followed. And they weren't the only ones. As the children walked to school, a long black sedan drove slowly along the curb about fifty yards behind them. Inside the car sat Misters 5, 29, 88, and 207.

"Well? Shall we nab 'em?" said Mr. 207 to Mr. 5, who was watching the children through high-powered binoculars.

"Nab them? Are you out of your mind? We can't afford to draw that kind of attention to ourselves. I swear, if it weren't for the fact that your uncle is Mr. 3, you'd be out on the street."

"Maybe I'll tell my uncle what you just said," Mr. 207 said smugly.

"Interesting," said Mr. 5, ignoring the threat. "Those earmuffs. I've never seen anything quite like them."

When Mr. Cheeseman first presented Jough with the earmuffs, made of a dark metal with a thin, coiled antenna protruding from each earpiece, Jough objected to having to wear them, thinking the other kids at school might make fun of him. Mr. Cheeseman argued that kids might be more likely to make fun of him if he were always falling down.

Jough considered this and agreed to wear the earmuffs on a trial basis. He found, to his surprise, that the children at his school were understanding and thoughtful to the point that none of them made fun of his odd-looking earmuffs.

"Look at those things. They look ridiculous," said Mr. 207, who lacked such thoughtfulness and understanding. "Kids today will put anything on their heads."

As Jough, Maggie, and Gerard neared the school, Jough stopped and turned around.

"What is it? What's wrong, Jough?" Maggie asked.

"I don't know," said Jough. "I just had a strange feeling. Like someone was spying on us."

"But we're just a bunch of normal kids," said Gerard. "Why would anybody want to spy on us?"

Jough shrugged. "You're right. Must be my imagination."

ETHAN'S SIMPLE YET DELICIOUS RECIPE FOR SQUASH

Ingredients

1 acorn squash
2 tablespoons butter
2 tablespoons firmly packed brown sugar
½ teaspoon cinnamon
⅛ teaspoon cloves
Two dozen frosted doughnuts

Instructions

Preheat oven to 375°F.

Cut squash in half lengthwise and remove fibers and seeds. Add butter, brown sugar, cinnamon, and cloves to the hollow scoop of each squash half. Place upright in the pan and roast for 20 to 30 minutes or until tender.

Remove squash from oven and place in garbage disposal.

Eat doughnuts.

Serves one.

CHAPTER 5

That Saturday, just three days after Agents El Kyoo and Aitch Dee first appeared on the Cheesemans' doorstep, a small brown car pulled up in front of the house. Behind the wheel of that little brown car was Pavel Dushenko, international superspy, his highly trained and highly puffy eyes locked on the small white house. Sitting next to him in the passenger seat was Leon, who had no last name. He had no last name because he was a chimp. This is not a way of saying he was a person lacking in refinement but rather a way of saying he was a chimpanzee, an ape.

Years earlier, while Pavel was on a secret mission in Khartoum, Leon saved his life. It all happened when Pavel slipped and fell out of a boat while traveling down the White Nile and was attacked by an angry hippopotamus, which, incidentally, is the worst type of hippopotamus by which to be attacked.

As the portly animal swam toward the equally portly superspy, the clever monkey cupped his hairy hands around his equally hairy mouth and shouted from the bank of the river, in perfect hippo, "Don't eat him. He's poisonous," which was potentially true considering that Pavel's diet included no fewer than three daily servings of ham.

Regardless, the hippo fell for the trick and Pavel was pulled, with great effort, back into the boat.

When he returned to his native country, Pavel brought his new friend with him, along with the idea that a highly trained chimp just might be the perfect complement to an international superspy. After all, Leon could climb over and under things that Pavel, with his ample waistline, could not. And in addition to his ability to speak perfect hippo, Leon could also do impressions of many other animals.

With great accuracy he could imitate: dogs, cats, donkeys, cows (both Holstein and Guernsey), lions, leopards, yaks, grizzly bears, polar bears, mole rats, baboons, hyenas, more than two hundred types of birds, and, on a good day, Jack Nicholson.

Pavel relied upon and trusted Leon more than any human he had ever met, which is why he allowed Leon to travel with his pet goldfish wherever they went, despite the fact that having a ten-gallon fish tank in the backseat of the car made the entire vehicle smell like low tide.

The three fish, named Goldie, Orangey, and Pete, were a birthday gift from Pavel to the monkey that had saved his life. They swam happily around the tank, which was plugged into the car's cigarette lighter in order to power the filter that kept the water clean, and the lights that enabled Leon to watch his little friends. This was something Leon could do for hours on end. The floor of the tank was decorated with brightly colored pebbles and was outfitted with several plastic trees and a miniature plastic replica of the Parthenon. The fish, Pete in particular, seemed to enjoy swimming in and out of the grooved plastic columns.

"We must get our hands on the LVR, Leon," said Pavel, speaking in his native tongue.

"Woo woo whaa," said Leon, speaking in his native chimp with a distinct lower east side Khartoum accent.

"Yes, you are right," said Pavel. "We will succeed simply because we are the best in all of world. We will get LVR by using incredible intelligence."

Leon showed that he was in full agreement by screaming and hitting himself repeatedly on the head.

Thirty minutes before that little brown car carrying an international superspy, a linguistically talented monkey, and three fishy-smelling fish pulled up in front of the Cheeseman house, Ethan and Olivia had gone off to a dinner party, the kind to which children are not invited. This was just fine with Jough, Maggie, and Gerard because the highlight of these so-called parties was something grown-ups like to call *conversation*.

And so the children happily remained at home and ate pizza, with Jough taking very seriously his temporary role as man of the house.

"Gerard, get your gum off the table."

His focus completely dedicated to the large slice of mushroom pizza before him, Gerard, without looking, removed the avocado-sized glob of chewing gum from the table and stuck it to his forehead.

"That's disgusting," said Maggie.

"Where else should I put it?" Gerard mumbled.

"How about the garbage can?"

Before Gerard could begin to explain how much time and effort it had taken to amass such an impressive wad of bubble gum and how foolish it would be to simply throw it away, the doorbell rang.

"I'll get it," said Jough in his man-of-the-house voice, a full octave lower than his regular voice. "You guys wait here."

Jough walked to the living room and looked through the peephole, where he saw, standing on the porch, a chubby man with puffy eyes holding what appeared to be a very large vacuum cleaner with a very large hose, perhaps ten inches in diameter. When Jough opened the door, he noticed that, standing next to the man, was a chimp.

"Good evening," said Pavel Dushenko, in the best English he could manage. "My pet minkey and I would like to demonstrate for you this dirt-sucking machine, which you will find to be very good and also not bad."

"That's okay," said Jough. "The . . . dirt-sucking machine we have works pretty well."

"Yes, maybe. But this one is very much more powerful," said Pavel. "You see here my friend Leon?"

Right on cue, Leon performed a curtsy, brief but with such aplomb as to be fitting for an audience with the queen.

"Yes," said Jough. "I see him."

"And do you see also his twin brother?"

"No, I don't," said Jough, looking from side to side. Leon also looked from side to side and shrugged.

"And do you know why that you do not see him?" asked Pavel.

"Uh . . . because he's not here?"

"Because he got very too close to this machine. *Whoomph.* Just like that, no more twin brother for Leon. Now, if only we could come inside your home and demonstrate—"

"I'm sorry," Jough interrupted. "My parents aren't home. Anyway, I don't think we really need a vacuum powerful enough to suck up a monkey."

"Is okay," Pavel countered. "Machine has many multiple settings. From musk ox all the way down to muskrat."

"We don't have any muskrats that need vacuuming either. Thanks anyway," said Jough as he pushed the door shut and locked it.

"Hmm," said Pavel dejectedly. "Brilliant plan to vacuum up LVR one piece at a time was perhaps not so brilliant."

Leon put his hands on his little monkey hips and shook his head.

"Who was it?" asked Maggie when Jough returned to the dinner table.

"Just a door-to-door salesman. And a monkey."

"What?" gasped Gerard. "A guy came to the door selling monkeys and you didn't buy one?"

"He wasn't selling monkeys. He was selling vacuum cleaners. The kind that can suck up a musk ox."

"What's a musk ox?" said Gerard, his face scrunched up in confusion. It was the scrunching of his face that caused the glob of bubble gum on his forehead to fall off onto his pizza.

"Congratulations," said Maggie. "You've just invented bubble gum–mushroom pizza."

"Cool," said Gerard.

As Pavel and Leon walked back toward the little brown car, lugging the giant dirt-sucking machine behind them, they were only partly surprised to find Agents El Kyoo and Aitch Dee waiting for them, leaning against the fender.

"Well, well, well," said Aitch Dee, his arms folded across his chest.

"Well, well, well, well," replied Pavel, not to be out welled.

"Look what we have here," said Aitch Dee, turning to El Kyoo. "Did you get a report of a couple of monkeys escaping from the zoo today?"

"No," said El Kyoo. "It was one monkey and one baboon, I believe."

Aitch Dee nodded and thought for a moment about smiling but quickly fought off the urge.

"Ha-ha. You are making me laugh so difficultly," said Pavel, who probably meant that El Kyoo was making him laugh so hard. Either way, he was not laughing at all and probably meant whatever he meant in the most sarcastic way possible.

"What are you up to, Dushenko?" El Kyoo demanded in an unwavering tone.

"What? We are only trying to make honest living, selling dirt-sucking machines door for door."

"You're here illegally and we're going to take you in and have you brought up on charges of espionage."

"Espionage?" scoffed Pavel. "That is ridiculous. I have my rights."

"You have the right to remain silent," said Aitch Dee as he took Pavel by the elbow. Pavel turned to Leon and shouted, "Musk ox!"

Leon quickly turned the setting on the large dirt-sucking machine to *musk ox*. With the sound of a jet engine, the machine fired up. Immediately the suction from the great hose drew in Aitch Dee's head with a resounding *whoomph*. If he had been a monkey, or a minkey for that matter, he would certainly have been sucked into the machine, never to be heard from again. Thankfully, his head was much larger than a monkey's, so the machine only swallowed his toupee, which, up to that point, had been a very well-kept secret.

El Kyoo yanked on the hose but only succeeded in pulling Aitch Dee around by the crown of his now-bald head.

"Turn it off!" yelled Aitch Dee in his usual steady voice, only louder. "Turn it off!"

In the meantime, Pavel and Leon were using the commotion as a chance to hop into their little brown car. As they sped away, Pavel leaned on the horn, stuck his head out the window, and yelled, "So very long, losers. See you next time."

Leon stuck his head out the opposite window and yelled, "Whaa whee waaah!"

As the car sped away, the goldfish sloshed happily around in the backseat.

CHAPTER 6

That Monday, Ethan and Olivia returned home after dropping the kids off at school to find a long white limousine with dark, tinted windows parked in front of their house.

When they walked inside, they were startled to see a small woman and a large man sitting in their living room. The large man had proportionally large hands and rings on every finger of his right hand, which held a brown leather briefcase. The woman was tight-lipped and had long red fingernails. She wore a ring as well, which bore a letter *P* made up of wavy blue lines. Ethan thought the wavy letter *P* looked very familiar.

With his non-ringed hand, the large man was petting Pinky's head, which at the time was still very scruffy, as most dogs' heads are. She enjoyed having her head rubbed nearly as much as she enjoyed drinking from the toilet and she sat there, wagging her tail happily. Pinky was not much of a watchdog in those days.

"What are you doing in our house?" Ethan demanded. "Who are you?"

"Relax, Mr. Cheeseman. We mean you no harm," said the small woman. "We're here to make you a very generous offer."

"If you're talking about the LVR, it's not for sale," said Ethan.

"Don't get excited here. We're not about to purchase some contraption that is half finished and that we have no idea how to operate. What we're offering, Mr. Cheeseman, is a job. A very high-paying job with considerable fringe benefits."

"And who is 'we,' exactly?"

"I work for a company called Plexiwave. Perhaps you've heard of it."

"I've heard of it," Olivia said. "You manufacture weapons. And we have no desire to have our inventions turned into something that might harm or kill people."

"You forget, Mrs. Cheeseman, we're also the world's leading manufacturer of refrigerators and microwave ovens."

Ethan now realized why the woman's ring looked so familiar. That same wavy letter P could be found on their microwave and their refrigerator in the kitchen.

"Well, our 'contraption,' as you say, will do nothing to keep food cold or heat up a frozen burrito," said Olivia.

"Don't be so naive, Mrs. Cheeseman," sneered the woman. "All great inventions will eventually be used to make weapons. I imagine the club was first invented as a means of cracking a nut. It was inevitable that one day it would be used for cracking skulls. That's just the way of the world, I'm afraid."

"Thank you, but we'll happily leave the business of skull cracking to people like you," said Olivia defiantly.

"How does two million dollars a year sound?" said the woman, ignoring what Olivia had just said.

"Two million dollars a year?" said Ethan.

"To start. With the first year's salary paid in advance."

The woman nodded to Mr. 29, who opened the briefcase revealing stacks and stacks of U.S. currency totaling what certainly looked to be two million dollars.

"Plus, you'll be entitled to benefits too numerous to list," the woman continued. "For starters, you and your family will be put up in a beautiful estate on a tropical island where the schools are second to none and there is absolutely no crime."

"The crime is people like you," Olivia shot back. "People like you devising new and innovative ways of hurting others and then selling that technology to the highest bidder. We will have no part of it, thank you."

Olivia walked over to the door and opened it.

"I will thank you to take your ill-gotten money, get back into your limo, and return to your factory of death," she asserted. "And furthermore, be advised that I fully intend to report you to the authorities."

With that, the small thin-lipped woman and the large man got up quietly and walked to the door.

"Very well," the woman said. "But I guarantee you've not heard the last of us."

The man and the woman walked out of the house and Olivia quickly slammed the door behind them and locked it.

"Well, that's it," Ethan said to Olivia. "I guess it's time for us to think about leaving."

"Leaving?" asked Olivia. "What do you mean?"

She looked out through the curtains and watched the man and the woman climb into the back of the limo as a driver in dark glasses held the door open for them.

"I mean we should pack up everything and move somewhere far away where nobody knows us. Someplace the children will be safe."

"I am not about to let those thugs force us out of our home. What kind of message is that for the children—that every time a bully confronts us, we run away? Now, just to be on the safe side I'm going to scramble the code to the LVR, in case it should fall into the wrong hands."

Ethan watched as his wife hurried off to her study. Maybe she was right, he thought. After all, she usually was. Maybe he was overreacting. Then again, daring to defy high-ranking officials from powerful multinational corporations like Plexiwave could be dangerous.

And, as Ethan would soon find out, it would be dangerous. In fact, it would be deadly.

"Headquarters," said the thin-lipped woman into her tiny cell phone as the limo sped away from the house.

"Headquarters. Go ahead, Ms. 4."

"Yes," said Ms. 4. "I need to speak to Mr. 1 immediately."

"Right away," said the woman at the other end.

Ms. 4 rode in silence as she waited a few moments until the deep, whispery voice of Mr. 1 came through the cell phone earpiece.

"Please tell me you were successful, Ms. 4," said Mr. 1.

"Not at this time, I'm afraid."

"And why not?"

"It's the woman," said Ms. 4. "I believe Mr. Cheeseman could be persuaded eventually. But his wife seems quite opposed to the idea."

"Then we must do something about that, mustn't we?" said Mr. 1.

"I understand," said Ms. 4. "I understand completely."

Several mornings later, Olivia awoke before the rest of the family and went downstairs to the kitchen, where she made a pot of coffee as she did every morning. Actually, to say she awoke before the rest of the family isn't entirely true, since to awaken you must first be asleep. Anxiety had been keeping Olivia up most nights since the encounter with the large man and the thin-lipped woman.

As the coffee brewed, she walked to the front door to fetch the newspaper. It was still dark outside and, for the first time in her life, she did not feel safe opening the door to her own house. She decided she would read the paper later and sat down to drink her coffee without it.

Not long after finishing her morning coffee, she began to feel ill. As she got the children up and ready for school, it got worse. She had a splitting headache and felt as though she might be running a fever. And so Olivia went off to see the doctor regarding her increasingly painful headache.

She sat in the waiting room, shielding her eyes from the bright fluorescent lights, until her name was called and she was told to wait for the doctor in the examining room. She waited for what seemed like a very long time until suddenly the door swung open and in walked a bald man with large reflective sunglasses and exceedingly shallow cheeks. His bare head glistened with sweat.

"Hello, Mrs. Cheeseman," he said. "What seems to be troubling you today?"

"You're not Dr. Spencer," she said.

"Well, there's nothing wrong with your vision," the man joked. "Dr. Spencer has gone home sick. Even we physicians aren't immune to a little sickness now and again."

With that he chuckled and pulled a tiny flashlight from his pocket.

"I'm Dr. Fiverson," the man said, shining the small light into each of Olivia's eyes.

"Dr. Fiverson?"

"Yes, it's . . . Swedish. Your eyes are very dilated. And you seem to be running a fever. I have just the thing for you."

The man calling himself Dr. Fiverson moved to the counter and began preparing a hypodermic needle.

"What is that?" Olivia asked.

"Something to help with your migraine," he said.

"But I never told you I had a migraine."

"Uh . . . yes. Well, before Dr. Spencer left for the day, he mentioned you had a history of migraines. And this is a new drug that works wonders on them."

And because this man said he was a colleague of their trusted family doctor, Olivia was only slightly suspicious of him. But she should have been much more suspicious. Especially when the doctor raised his arm to inject her with whatever was in that hypodermic needle. Because when he did, his sleeve rode up, revealing a strange tattoo on his left wrist. A tattoo that read *3VAW1X319*. And if she had seen that tattoo reflected in his mirrored sunglasses, she surely would have run from the room and gone straight to the police. For when seen in a mirror, that strange tattoo read *Plexiwave.*

ADVICE ON CHOOSING A DOCTOR

There comes a time in everyone's life (being born, for instance) when he or she will require the help of a qualified physician. When this time does arrive, you'll want to make sure you end up with a good one because, for one thing, doctors aren't cheap.

Gone are the days when the old country doctor would drive out to your house and amputate your infected leg in exchange for a basket of goose eggs and a rhubarb pie.

Nowadays, such a procedure would cost you quite a bit more. By the time you managed to bake enough rhubarb pies, your leg would probably fall off by itself.

At today's prices, you can't afford to entrust your health and well-being to anyone but the best doctors available. I have therefore put together a short list of warning signs to indicate that perhaps you have selected a bad doctor.

☆ He listens to your heart by holding a drinking glass to your chest.

☆ The skeleton in his office has one arm.

☆ The aquarium in the waiting room contains two or more dead fish.

☆ He advises you to drink plenty of solids.

☆ He has a sweaty, bald head and a tattoo on his left wrist that, when seen in a mirror, forms the name of an evil international weapons conglomerate.

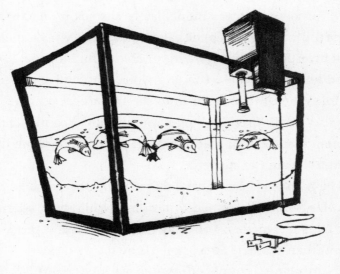

CHAPTER 7

Olivia returned from the clinic feeling worse than she had before she went in. She told her husband about the substitute doctor with the strange tattoo who had given her the injection.

Mr. Cheeseman was immediately suspicious, and when Olivia drifted off to sleep, he called the police, who launched a full investigation but were never able to find the man who called himself Dr. Fiverson or anyone who had ever heard of him. When Ethan went in to see the officer assigned to the case, a tall, tired-looking man with a calico mustache, the man assured him that they were doing everything they could to locate the suspect.

The man was friendly and offered Mr. Cheeseman a cup of coffee, which he served to him in a white mug adorned with a letter *P* made up of wavy blue lines. This is precisely when Ethan realized he was on his own.

Over the next couple of months, various specialists prescribed various medications but Olivia's condition failed to improve. At one point, she became bedridden. She passed the time by knitting things for her children when she could muster up the strength. In addition to being a fabulous cook, a wonderful mother, and a brilliant scientist, Olivia could knit just about anything. Give her enough yarn and it was quite possible she could knit a go-cart or a grand piano. But she was too weak for projects of such enormity and so she kept it simple. For Jough, she made a stocking cap, for Maggie, a lovely scarf, and for little Gerard, a sock puppet, which he immediately named Steve, placed on his left hand, and vowed never to remove.

In time, Olivia's energy diminished to the point that even holding her knitting needles was too difficult, and the many medications she was taking turned something as simple as knitting into a frustrating and confusing endeavor.

Powerless to help her, Ethan could only sit and watch as his beautiful wife, the love of his life, slowly slipped into unconsciousness, never to waken again.

ADVICE ON BEING A GOOD MOTHER

Knit stocking caps, scarves, and sock puppets named Steve.

CHAPTER 8

Until Mr. Cheeseman is able to complete work on the LVR, the only way to travel through time is with a handy literary device known as the flashback or, in this case, the flash-forward, for here we are nearly two years after the death of the lovely Olivia, two years since Ethan and his children first went underground, and they are still on the run from people like Mr. 5, Ms. 4, international superspy Pavel Dushenko, and a top secret government agency. More important, the LVR, the only means of ever seeing their mother alive again, is still not working.

"What do you think the problem is?" asked Jough as the station wagon made its way down the rural highway and Gerard periodically stuck his head out the window and mooed at herds of unsuspecting cows.

"The problem, scientifically speaking, is the code," said Mr. Cheeseman. "Wisely, your mother encrypted it to keep it safe. She wrote it out on a piece of paper and recently I've been able to decipher it. The problem is, it's only half there."

With that, Mr. Cheeseman removed a mint green piece of paper from his breast pocket and handed it to Jough, whose forehead immediately wrinkled. The paper had obviously been torn down the middle.

"It does seem to be only half there," he said. "What do you think happened to the other half?"

"I don't know. Lost, I suppose."

"May I see it?" said Maggie from the backseat. "I'm pretty good at solving puzzles and things."

Jough handed the paper back over his shoulder to his sister. Unlike Jough, her forehead did not wrinkle up when she read it. Instead, her eyes darted back and forth across the paper, seemingly searching for something in the code, which took the form of a sentence or, rather, an incomplete sentence. It read *When danger lurks and your heart is racing . . .*

"Well," said Maggie. "It seems that this is the first line of a piece of advice. Advice on what to do when danger lurks. To figure out the rest, all we need to do is complete the sentence."

"Very interesting," said Mr. Cheeseman. "I think you may be on to something. Why don't you read the first part again and we'll each take a crack at completing the sentence."

"I'll go first," said Jough, eager to show that he was every bit as smart as his younger sister.

"Me second," said Gerard, loudly working the bubble gum.

"Me third," said Steve.

"Grrrr," said Pinky to the one-eyed sock puppet.

Maggie cleared her throat, not because it needed clearing but because she wanted to make sure she had the undivided attention of everyone in the car.

"When danger lurks and your heart is racing . . . ," she read.

Jough thought for a moment before blurting out, "Run!"

"Run?" said Maggie. "Seriously, does that sound like the kind of advice Mom would've given us? In the face of danger we should run?"

"Well, isn't that what we've been doing?"

"Well, yes," admitted Maggie. "I guess that's true."

"Still," said Mr. Cheeseman, "it's too short. The completed code should contain at least fifty figures."

"How about run and hide?" Gerard offered.

"Still too short," said Mr. Cheeseman.

"How about run and hide in the basement?" said Steve. "Behind some boxes . . . under the stairs . . . at night . . . with a fake wig and dark glasses?"

"Well, I can certainly give that a try, Steve. As soon as we get to where we're going. In the meantime, keep thinking about it. Maybe one of you will figure it out."

"I bet it'll be me," said Gerard. "I just have one question. What does *lurks* mean?"

Gerard did not receive an answer to his question. He did not receive an answer because anyone in the car who could have answered it was looking up ahead at the strange bus parked on the side of the road next to an open field. It looked like an old school bus in all ways but the color. This school bus was black with the words *Captain Jibby's Traveling Circus Sideshow* painted across its side in large white letters.

Not in the best of shape, the bus had bald tires and the radio antenna had been replaced with a wire coat hanger. The gas cap was also missing and in its place was an old rag stuffed into the opening, giving the bus the look of a four-thousand-pound black-and-white Molotov cocktail on wheels. The hood was open and a man was standing on a wooden apple box next to the bus, leaning over the engine. He looked a little like a lion tamer with his head in the mouth of a large black lion with white lettering across its side.

"Looks like somebody's having engine trouble," said Mr. Cheeseman as he slowed the car.

"But Dad," said Jough. "You're not going to stop, are you? I mean, who knows how far behind us they are."

"We must never allow our own circumstances to become an excuse for not helping others in need," said Mr. Cheeseman. "Besides, I'm sure we could all use the opportunity to stretch our legs a bit."

"You can say that again," said Steve.

"And furthermore," added Mr. Cheeseman, "if danger lurks, I'm sure Pinky will let us know."

"What does *lurks* mean?" Gerard repeated his question.

"It means that it's hiding, ready to pounce at a moment's notice," said Maggie with an intentionally creepy look on her face. "In fact, it could be right behind you and you'd never even know it. Look out!"

Gerard screamed and spun around to look where Maggie

was pointing, but there was nothing there. Maggie laughed at her little brother.

"That wasn't funny," said Gerard. "Dad, tell Maggie it's not funny to scare people."

"Please don't scare your brother," said Mr. Cheeseman as he pulled the station wagon in behind the bus.

"Okay, Dad," Maggie agreed, reluctantly, for it was hard to commit to giving up something that could be so much fun.

Pinky and the children climbed out of the car and followed Mr. Cheeseman to the front of the bus, where the man under the hood was grunting and mumbling a string of words that, if used by a child, would certainly result in that child having his or her mouth washed out with soap.

Mr. Cheeseman cleared his throat loudly in an attempt to alert the man to their presence and perhaps put a stop to all the cursing.

The man rose up quickly, smacking the back of his head on the engine's hood. Just as he was about to launch into a veritable greatest hits of swearing, he turned to see Mr. Cheeseman and his three young children.

"Oh. Ahoy there," said the large man, his thick Scottish accent pushing its way through his bushy orange beard. "What can I do for you fine folks?"

"Actually, it appears that you might be the one who could use some help," said Mr. Cheeseman.

"Huh? Oh, yes. That I am," said the man with a hearty laugh as he stepped off the wooden box. Even without the help of the box, the man stood more than a half-foot taller than Mr. Cheeseman. He wore a tattered blue jacket with tarnished brass buttons down the front and on the sleeves, which were stained with no small amount of engine grease. In his right hand, he appeared to be holding a Swiss Army knife with the screwdriver extended.

"Pardon my manners," the large man said. "My name is Jibby."

"As in Captain Jibby?" Maggie asked.

"Aye," the man said. "That be me all right."

"I'm Ethan," Mr. Cheeseman offered. "And this is Jough, Maggie, and Gerard."

Each of Mr. Cheeseman's three attractive, polite, and relatively odor-free children smiled and nodded as he or she was introduced.

Steve cleared his throat loudly.

"Oh yes," continued Mr. Cheeseman. "This is Steve. And that is Pinky."

Pinky did not smile and nod politely. She was busy sniffing Jibby's shoes.

"Well, I must say it's a pleasure to meet you all," said Jibby, offering his new friends a crisp salute. As his right hand snapped to his forehead, it became apparent that he was not holding a Swiss Army knife but rather that the knife had been somehow attached to his wrist where one's hand might normally be. The children couldn't help but stare.

"Would you like me to take a look at it?" said Mr. Cheeseman, nodding toward the bus. "I'm quite handy with most kinds of machines."

"If you don't mind," said Jibby. "I've been messin'

around with it for two hours now with not so much as a snifter full of luck."

"Our dad can fix anything," Gerard said proudly. "He's an inventor."

Maggie gave Gerard a stern look and elbowed him in the ribs.

"What happened, exactly?" Mr. Cheeseman asked Jibby.

"Well, we were cruisin' down the road nigh about fifty knots, when suddenly—"

"Knots?" said Mr. Cheeseman.

"Sorry. Fifty miles per hour. When suddenly she started to make a racket that would wake the dead. Then the old girl just up and quit on me. We coasted to the side of the road and, like I said, that was over two hours ago."

"I'll see what I can find," said Mr. Cheeseman as he climbed up onto the apple box and stuck his head beneath the hood.

The children stood in silence for a few moments until Gerard could take it no longer.

"You have a Swiss Army knife instead of a hand," he blurted out. Again, Maggie nudged her little brother sharply in the ribs.

"Really," she scolded. "That's rude. I'm sorry, Mr. Jibby. Please excuse my brother. He can be pretty obnoxious sometimes."

"First of all," said Jibby, "let's forget all this Mister nonsense. The name is Jibby, plain and simple. Or Captain if you like. Second of all, there ain't no reason to apologize for pointin' out the obvious."

Jibby looked at his right hand with a certain pride and admiration. With his left hand he snapped the screwdriver back into the knife's handle.

"It is indeed a knife," he said. "And she's served me well over the years. You know, when I first lost my hand, they wanted to replace it with a hook. Can you imagine that? An ordinary, everyday hook? So I got to thinkin'. Why not replace it with something more useful? Now, the first thought I had was a can opener. That's a handy item to have."

Maggie and Jough smirked.

"What's so funny?" asked Jibby.

"You said a can opener would be a *handy* item to have," said Maggie.

"Yes?" said Jibby. "And what's so funny about that?"

Maggie and Jough looked at each other, not sure whether Jibby was pulling their legs.

"You see, Jibby," Jough started. "Well, it's just that, you lost your hand and you said a can opener would be . . ."

Jough decided in midsentence not to continue, based on the look of utter confusion on Jibby's bristly face.

"Never mind. Please . . . continue your story."

"Yes, anyway," said Jibby. "I then thought that perhaps a pair of scissors might be a more versatile item. I imagined a screwdriver might be good as well. Then I thought, why not all of the above and more. And that's how I ended up with this."

"And how did you lose your hand?" asked Gerard, whose

mouth seemed to be directly connected to Maggie's elbow, as it poked him sharply in the ribs once more.

"Hey," Gerard protested.

"That, my lad, is a good question," Jibby said, kneeling on one knee in front of Gerard. "Now let me ask you one. Do know the proper way to feed a tiger a slab of raw meat?"

"No," said Gerard.

"Well, neither do I," said Jibby with a laugh so forceful it seemed as though it must have hurt. He punctuated the laugh by slapping his left hand on his thigh. This time it was the children's turn to be left out of the joke. Having your hand eaten by a tiger didn't seem the least bit funny to them even if the person whose hand was eaten found it so.

"Was your hand really eaten by a tiger?" asked Gerard.

"Was indeed," said Jibby, rising to his full six and a half feet. "Was a time that the sideshow traveled with a host of exotic animals. Two Bengal tigers, a crocodile, a giant python, and a Tibetan yak that stood six feet at the shoulder. Beautiful creatures they were. And talented too, I might add. The tigers could ride unicycles."

"Wow," marveled Gerard.

"What happened to them?" asked Maggie.

"Well," said Jibby as Mr. Cheeseman continued to fiddle away under the hood of the broken-down bus, "I soon realized that a traveling sideshow is no place for a wild animal. The beasts, I'm afraid, were very unhappy. So I did what any kindhearted person would do. I set them free."

"You mean, you released them back into the jungle?" asked Jough.

"Jungle?" said Jibby with another painfully hearty laugh. "Why, there's no jungle anywhere near here."

The children looked at one another once again, not sure what to make of this latest bit of information.

"You mean you just . . . let them go? Here?" said Jough.

"Well, not here," said Jibby. "I believe it was Utah."

"Utah?" said Maggie. "You let two Bengal tigers loose in the middle of Utah?"

"Two Bengal tigers, a crocodile, a giant python, and a Tibetan yak," said Jibby. "But now that I think about it, it could just as easily have been Vermont. Anyway, now our little traveling show is made up of people only. Strange people, yes, but people nonetheless. We're on our way to Hollywood, you know, to try and break into the movies. How about you folks? Where you headed?"

"Anywhere but Utah or Vermont," said Steve.

CHAPTER 9

"I think I may have found your problem," said Mr. Cheese-man as he emerged from beneath the hood, holding what looked like a twisted, mangled fencing sword. It looked like a twisted, mangled fencing sword because that's exactly what it was.

"Is that a sword?" asked Gerard.

"It was," said Jibby, taking it from Mr. Cheeseman. "It belongs to Jake, our sword swallower."

"I think he'd have a hard time swallowing that one," said Jough.

"Not if I rammed it down his throat he wouldn't," said Jibby. "He's always leaving his things lying around. And now it's cost us two full hours of travel time and one big headache."

"Not to mention a really nice sword," said Maggie.

"By the way," said Jough. "Where is Jake? And where are the rest of your performers?"

"Sleeping in the bus, if I know them. The lousy layabouts." Jibby scowled. "I'll summon them right away so they can offer you the proper thanks for your very generous help."

"That's not necessary," said Mr. Cheeseman. "We were more than happy to do it. Besides, we all needed to stretch our legs."

"Well, I wouldn't feel right if you didn't give us the opportunity to repay you somehow," said Jibby. "Are you hungry?"

"Starving," said Gerard.

"Yes, starving," echoed Steve.

"Then you shall stay for supper," said Jibby in a tone that was not to be argued with. "I can say with complete confidence that our cook, the lovely Juanita, is the best cook of any traveling circus sideshow working today."

"How many traveling circus sideshows are there working today?" asked Maggie.

"Hmm," said Jibby. "If I had to guess, I'd say . . . one. But trust me when I say Juanita's cooking is world class."

"We wouldn't want her to go to any trouble," said Mr. Cheeseman.

"Trouble?" boomed Jibby. "It would be her pleasure. In fact, I believe that tonight, in your honor, Captain Jibby's Traveling Circus Sideshow will throw a good old-fashioned wingding."

Jibby laughed and clapped his hands together in unbridled delight.

"Excuse me," said Gerard, tugging on Jibby's heavily buttoned sleeve. "What's a wingding?"

"What's a wingding? Why, a wingding is, uh . . . it's just like a shindig but without all the hullabaloo. Now, let's meet the rest of the group, shall we?"

Jibby yanked open the bus door and climbed on board.

"All right, listen up and listen up good. Tonight, we're puttin' on a regular wingding in honor of our new friends who were kind enough to stop and help us out. So get your lazy backsides up and get ready to do some work for a change."

Jough looked at Maggie and Ethan. Ethan shrugged, causing Jough and Maggie to smile.

"Tonight, we'll have a feast like no other," said Jibby as he climbed off the bus. "And entertainment that will leave you breathless."

"Really?" said Gerard.

With this, Jibby sighed heavily and looked to the dirt beneath his feet.

"Well," he started. "Not exactly, I'm afraid. There was a time when we were something to behold. But in recent years, I must admit we've lost a bit of our edge."

"We don't mind," said Maggie with a smile. "Being left breathless is highly overrated."

"Yeah," said Jough. "Besides, I'm sure you're just being modest."

"If you think I'm being modest, then you don't know me very well," said Jibby with a snort.

The first to make his way off the bus was a short, chubby man with a blue and white bandanna tied around his head. What was even more noticeable about the man, however, was that he wore glasses and, beneath those glasses, over his left eye, was a large black eye patch.

"Ah, there you are," said Jibby angrily. "Been lookin' for this?"

Jibby thrust the mangled sword at the man in the bandanna.

"My best swallowing sword," said the man in a low, sandpapery voice. "Where did you find it?"

Jibby looked to Mr. Cheeseman, who said, "Actually, I found it. It was wrapped around the fan belt. I'm Ethan, by the way. And these are my children: Jough, Maggie, and Gerard."

Steve cleared his throat.

"And that's Steve."

"Pleasure to meet you," said the man, offering a slight bow.

"You must be Jake, the sword swallower," said Maggie.

"Three-Eyed Jake is my name, sword swallowin's my game."

"Excuse me, sir," said Gerard. "But why do they call you Three-Eyed Jake?"

"Why do they call me Three-Eyed Jake? Well, I'll tell ya why. When I first got my spectacles here, people started calling me Four Eyes. 'Hey, here comes old Four Eyes,' they'd say. Then, when I lost my left eye, well, four minus one equals—"

"Three!" Gerard interrupted.

"Right," said Three-Eyed Jake, reaching out and roughing up Gerard's spiky hair. "Smart as a whip, this one is."

"But how did you lose your eye?" asked Gerard, making certain he was out of range of Maggie's elbow.

"Bit of advice," said Jake. "Never practice sword swallowing if you're farsighted and you've misplaced your glasses."

The children winced at the thought of it. Even Steve winced with his solitary eye.

"I had a glass eye for a while," said Jake wistfully. "Beautiful thing it was. Haven't a clue as to where I might have left the darn thing."

"You'd lose your head if it wasn't attached to your neck," said Jibby.

"Reminds me . . . almost lost my head once, too," said Jake. "All over a beautiful woman and a bottle of rye."

Jibby reached out and smacked Jake on the back of his head.

"Is that an appropriate story for children?"

"No," said Jake. "I suppose it ain't."

"Right. Now run off and start setting up for a feast to remember."

"Aye, Captain," he said with a salute.

As Jake walked toward the back of the bus, another man, tall and thin with a simple expression on his face, stumbled off the bus.

"Everybody, this here's Dizzy," said Jibby. "Dizzy's our tightrope walker."

"Hello, Dizzy," said Mr. Cheeseman with his hand extended. "I'm Ethan."

Dizzy shook Mr. Cheeseman's hand but said nothing.

"Don't take offense," said Jibby. "He can't talk."

"You mean he's mute?" Jough asked.

"Mute?" said Jibby. "I wish. No, he has the ability to speak, that's for darned sure. He just can't because, frankly, I won't let him. So many stupid things have come out of his mouth over the years that finally one day I completely revoked his speaking privileges. That was four years ago."

"You mean he hasn't spoken in four years?" asked Jough.

"Not to me he hasn't," confirmed Jibby.

"I can think of at least one other person who should have his speaking privileges revoked," said Maggie, nodding toward her little brother.

"If I had my way, it'd be half the world's population," said Jibby with a smile and a wink before turning to address Dizzy. "Now listen, Dizzy. We're throwing a wingding for our new friends here. So let's get to work setting it all up."

As Dizzy nodded and turned to leave, a look of inspiration suddenly washed across Jibby's face.

"Wait! You know, now that I think about it, forget the wingding. Let's go all out and make it a shindig. Why not? A shindig it is. Which means there's plenty of hullabaloo to take care of, so let's get going."

Dizzy smiled his simple smile, then zigzagged toward the back of the bus, where Three-Eyed Jake was busy pulling folding chairs and banquet tables from the storage compartment.

"I don't mean to be rude," said Jough. "But Dizzy seems like kind of a weird name for a tightrope walker."

Jibby breathed out a sigh of exhaustion.

"Not in this case it's not," he said. "That's the problem with our whole operation here. It's all fallin' apart. Our strong man hurt his back and couldn't lift a feather. Our fortune teller got hit on the head and suffers from short-term memory loss. Can't remember predictions he made two minutes before. And three weeks ago I had to fire both Wolf Boy and the Fat Lady."

"Why did you have to fire them?" Gerard mumbled through his giant plug of bubble gum.

"Because the darn fools went and fell in love with each other," said Jibby bitterly.

"Sorry, but what's wrong with that?" Mr. Cheeseman wondered.

"I have a very strict policy against employees dating," said Jibby. "Ever since that tragedy last year with the Bearded Lady and the Human Torch. Anyway, try gettin' people to fork over their hard-earned money to see a strong man with a back injury, a fortune teller with short-term memory loss, and a tightrope walker with vertigo."

Jough turned to Mr. Cheeseman.

"Dad?" he said. "What about the earmuffs?"

"I don't know," said Mr. Cheeseman. "Are you sure you don't need them?"

"I'm sure, Dad. I've been completely cured of that. I haven't fallen down in over six months."

"Okay," said Mr. Cheeseman. "Run and get them."

Jough ran back to the station wagon with Pinky right behind him.

"I'm not sure about the others," said Mr. Cheeseman. "But perhaps we can help your tightrope walker with his balancing problem."

SOME UP-FRONT ADVICE ON AVOIDING BACK INJURIES

Always lift with your legs, no matter how tempting it might be to use your hands.

CHAPTER 10

Mr. Cheeseman and his three children sat at a long banquet table and watched in wonder as everyone rushed about to set up a fabulous shindig complete with all the hullabaloo. Well, not everyone helped. Sammy the strong man, whose back was too sore to be doing anything, sat and watched as well.

Sammy was a dark man with a long brown ponytail and enormous arms, similar in circumference to the trunk of your average sycamore.

"I'm one-half Cherokee," he explained in a soft and easy voice that belied the man's brutish appearance. "One-half Cherokee, one-half Irish, one-half Turkish, one-half Australian, and one-half Korean."

"Excuse me, but that's five halves," said Maggie.

"Yes. That's why I have the strength of two and a half men. Or at least I used to," he said sadly. "I once lifted a horse over my head, you know. Not a pony, a full-grown horse. A full-grown horse that had just eaten a big meal.

I don't think he liked it very much, but the crowd went wild. Boy, those were the days."

"What happened to your back?" Gerard questioned before blowing a large pink bubble.

"Well, having the strength of two and a half men can be very stressful. People are always asking you to lift things. 'Bet you can't lift that pool table,' they'll say. Or, 'Hey, let's see you lift that pinball machine with one hand.' It's just too much pressure."

"That doesn't explain how you hurt your back," said Maggie.

"Sure it does. All the stress started to give me nightmares," said Sammy as though that would suffice.

"I'm sorry," said Maggie. "But I still don't see how a nightmare can result in a back injury."

"Well, let me ask you this," said Sammy. "Have you ever seen a movie or a television show where one of the characters is lying in bed having a terrible nightmare? Then suddenly he wakes up and bolts upright in bed screaming, with his face covered in sweat? Well, the same thing happened to me, except I was sleeping on my stomach."

Mr. Cheeseman and his children winced.

"Ouch," said Maggie.

"Ouch is right," said Sammy. "My back hasn't been the same since."

"Pardon me for saying so," said Mr. Cheeseman, "but it seems as though just about every member of your troupe here suffers from some type of physical affliction. Jibby's missing a hand, Jake has lost an eye, Dizzy is, well, dizzy, and you've sustained what appears to be a very serious back injury."

"Yes," whispered Sammy. "It's the curse."

"What curse?" Gerard whispered back.

"I'm afraid that's all I can say about it," said Sammy mysteriously. "If I say any more, Jibby's liable to take away my speaking privileges. And having the strength of two and a half men is stressful enough without losing my speaking privileges on top of that."

"Have you tried breathing exercises?" asked Maggie.

"Breathing hardly seems like much exercise," said Sammy. "Anything you can do in your sleep can't be considered exercise, can it?"

"No, I mean using deep breathing and meditation as a way to relieve stress and to relax your muscles. My mother taught me. I'd be happy to show you. It might help with your stress and with your chronic back pain."

"At this point I'm willing to try anything," said Sammy. "Even something as crazy as breathing."

When Jibby and his crew had finished setting up, they took their seats at the banquet tables and prepared to take part in a feast like no other, prepared by Juanita, an olive-skinned beauty with a soft, white smile.

Gracefully, she glided from table to table, dishing up generous portions of delicious foods from around the world: empanadas, goulash, souvlaki, and udon noodles.

"*Hay un montón de alimento. Coma tanto como usted quiere,*" she said, which meant, "There is a mountain of food. Eat as much as you like."

It was absolutely the best meal Mr. Cheeseman and his children had eaten in almost two years. Though a certifiable genius when it came to the ways of inventing useful objects, Mr. Cheeseman, unlike his beautiful wife, was no cook.

"This food is delicious," said Jough.

"You sure were right about Juanita," said Maggie to Jibby, who was sitting at the next table over.

"We may be knaves, but we eat like kings," said Jibby, his fiery beard dappled with gourmet crumbs.

"She seems nice. She reminds me of Mom," said Jough, watching Juanita as she filled the plates of the hungry crew.

"She may be nice, but Mom was even nicer. And even prettier," said Gerard sadly. "I wish she were here right now. When is that stupid time machine going to be finished anyway?"

Silence fell over the table. Mr. Cheeseman dropped his fork. Jough and Maggie shot Gerard a look of horror.

Three-Eyed Jake moved his eyes to the left to find Jibby looking back at him. He then turned his three eyes back toward Gerard.

"Pardon me, lad. But did you say something about a time machine?"

Gerard looked to his father, not knowing what to say.

"No, no, no," Mr. Cheeseman interrupted. "He didn't say time machine. He said . . . dime machine."

"A dime machine?" said Jake skeptically.

"Yes, you know. Like nickels and dimes."

"I see. And just what does a dime machine do?"

"Well, it uh . . . it counts your dimes for you," said Mr. Cheeseman.

"Yes," said Jough. "I can't wait until that dime machine is up and working. I've got this big jar full of dimes but I have no idea how many are in there."

"You will just as soon as that dime machine is finished," said Maggie.

"Yes," said Mr. Cheeseman. "Should be done in a matter of time. I mean, in a matter of . . . weeks. So anyway, we should probably be going soon. It'll be dark in a couple of hours and we need to find a place to stay for the night."

"Well, you can't leave yet," said Jibby. "You've gotta stay for the entertainment. Look!"

Jibby pointed up into the sky with his right hand. All eyes followed the bright red handle of the Swiss Army knife to see Dizzy, standing on the crossbar of a telephone pole near the roadside. In his hands he held a long wooden balancing stick and, on his head, Jough's specially designed balancing earmuffs.

"It's Dizzy," Gerard exclaimed. "He's gonna walk on the wire."

"I don't know if that's such a good idea," said Mr. Cheeseman to Sammy. "The way your luck is running around here, he's liable to get electrocuted."

"Wouldn't be the first time," said Sammy.

Dizzy took a deep breath and slowly slid his right foot out onto the wire. Following another deep breath, he slid his left foot out behind it. A look of relief washed over his face and soon turned into a smile. He lifted his left foot and placed it in front of his right. With each step, he gained more and more confidence until he was practically strolling across that wire.

When he reached the opposite side, the group let out a cheer. Mr. Cheeseman and his children rose to their feet to give Dizzy a standing ovation.

"Wow," exclaimed Gerard. "Did you see that? I want to be a tightrope walker when I grow up."

And the entertainment didn't stop there. After dinner, Three-Eyed Jake put on a sword-swallowing demonstration that left young Gerard in utter awe, especially when he swallowed two swords at once.

"I want to be a sword swallower when I grow up," Gerard declared.

Hearing this seemed to make Three-Eyed Jake very happy.

"Let me tell you somethin', Gerard. Swallow a sword and it'll change your whole outlook on life. Because once you do, nothing else seems that difficult."

While Maggie taught Sammy a series of relaxation and breathing exercises and Three-Eyed Jake gave Gerard a tutorial in the fine art of sword swallowing, Jough and Mr. Cheeseman were being introduced to the fortune teller.

"Ethan? Jough?" said Jibby. "This is the Amazing Aristotle."

"No relation," said Aristotle, as he did any time he was introduced. "I'm no philosopher. I make no comment on the nature of things. It's only my job to foresee them before they come to pass."

Aristotle was a sturdy man with shiny black eyes, his arms and chest decorated with thick black hair. His bushy eyebrows looked like something you might use to scour a pot. Numerous dark green tattoos hid beneath the jungle of wiry black hair carpeting his forearms.

"Prepare to be amazed by my incredible psychic powers," he said in an overly dramatic voice as he sat down at a small folding table cluttered with charts and maps of the night sky. Jough and Ethan sat down opposite him.

"Okay, now where were we?" asked Aristotle.

"We were preparing to be amazed," said Jough, who was not certain exactly how to prepare for such a thing.

"Right," said Aristotle. "And amazed you shall be. Psychic ability is a very rare attribute indeed. Now where were we?"

"Psychic ability is a very rare attribute indeed," repeated Mr. Cheeseman.

"You can say that again," said Aristotle. As the psychic studied the maps before him, Jough looked at Ethan and both fought the urge to laugh at the absurdity of it all.

"So, let me ask you. Is this your first encounter with a real live amazing psychic?"

"Actually, our dog is psychic," said Jough.

Mr. Cheeseman used a small cough to hide the snicker that escaped his lips.

"What?" gasped Aristotle. "A dog that can predict the future! Do you dare mock the Amazing Aristotle?"

"No, of course not," said Jough. "Our dog really is psychic. I mean, she can't predict the future, but she's able to warn us any time danger is nearby."

"She got her psychic powers by drinking from the toilet," said Mr. Cheeseman. "How did you get yours?"

"Certainly not by drinking from the toilet," said Aristotle.

"Oh no, of course not," said Mr. Cheeseman. "I didn't mean to imply that. I was just curious, that's all."

"You mean curious as in fascinated?" said Aristotle.

"Yes," said Jough quickly. "That's exactly it."

"Then prepare to be fascinated. Now where were we?"

"I think you were going to tell us our future," Jough said.

"Yes, the future."

Aristotle gazed at the well-wrinkled charts before him, then spoke in the direction of Mr. Cheeseman.

"I see you dancing with a beautiful woman. You are very happy."

"Dad," said Jough excitedly. "Do you think it's Mom?"

"I don't know," said Mr. Cheeseman. "What does she look like?"

"What does who look like?" said Aristotle.

Suddenly, the sounds of music struck the air. Jough and Mr. Cheeseman looked over to see Jibby standing near the bus and playing a fiddle, the bow clasped between the scissors of his Swiss Army hand.

The men in the group all leaped to their feet, clapping and stomping right along with Jibby. They took turns dancing with Juanita, her long pleated skirt twirling about like a red and green parachute. She first danced with Jake and Dizzy, then with Sammy, whose back seemed to be doing much better.

Mr. Cheeseman smiled as he watched. His smile caught

Juanita's eye and she twirled her way over to the table, offering him her hand. Suddenly Mr. Cheeseman's smile disappeared. As lovely as Juanita was, all he could think about was what a fabulous dancer Olivia had been. Mr. Cheeseman looked at his son.

"Jough?" he asked.

With only one word, Jough knew what his father meant.

"Sure, Dad," said Jough, and he stood up, took Juanita's hand, and danced with her until Jibby's tired arm could fiddle no more.

CHAPTER 11

With darkness closing in, it was time for Mr. Cheeseman and his family to bid farewell to their new friends, quite certain, as with everyone else they had befriended over the last two and a half years, that they would never see them again.

"That was, without a doubt, the best shindig I've ever been a part of," said Mr. Cheeseman to the entire group as they gathered around the station wagon to say their good-byes. "Thank you all very much."

"Nonsense," said Jibby. "It is we who should be thanking you. Some of us more than others. In fact, I think Dizzy's got something to say to you."

Dizzy looked at Jibby, not sure what to make of this.

"That's right," said Jibby. "In honor of this happy occasion, I'm reinstating your speaking privileges."

With a smile and a sigh of relief, Dizzy turned to Mr. Cheeseman and his family and spoke for the first time in four years. His words came slowly and seemed to stretch out to the point that they might break.

"Before today," he began, "I was useless. Helpless. But thanks to you, I can stand on my own two feet again. Or on one foot. On a single wire. Thirty feet above the ground. I don't know how to thank you."

"Just don't forget us when you become a big star in Hollywood," said Maggie.

"Don't worry about that," said Jibby. "Ain't none of us going to forget you folks. Well, none of us but Aristotle here. Half the time he can't remember his own name."

"Have you tried bubble gum?" asked Gerard.

"Bubble gum?" said Aristotle.

"Yes, chewing bubble gum. I don't know why, but it always helps me to remember stuff."

"It's been scientifically shown to improve memory and concentration," said Maggie as if she had known that all along.

"Here," said Gerard, reaching into his pants pocket and removing a package of bubble gum that looked as though someone had been sitting on it for several hours, which indeed someone had.

"I've got more, so you can have this. Even if it doesn't work for you, it's fun to chew. You can even put it on pizza."

Aristotle seemed genuinely touched by the offer.

"Thank you," he said, reaching out with his heavily decorated arm and gently taking the flattened pack of gum from Gerard.

"Well then," said Jibby as he stepped forward and produced a business card. The card was black and read *Captain Jibby's Traveling Circus Sideshow* in the same white lettering that adorned the side of the bus. "Here's my card should you ever find yourself in need of anything. And I mean anything. Call me day or night."

"Thanks, Jibby," said Mr. Cheeseman, taking the card.

"I'd like one too," said Maggie.

Jibby laughed and pulled several cards from his pocket.

"You can all have one," he said, passing them out to Jough, Maggie, and Gerard.

Right then, Pinky let out a low, rumbling growl and it was not directed at Steve.

"Uh-oh, Dad," said Jough. "Did you hear that?"

"Sure did. Are you certain, Pinky?"

"Grrrrrr," growled Pinky.

"What's wrong with the little hairless beast?" asked Jibby.

"Uh . . . nothing," said Mr. Cheeseman. "She's just anxious to get back on the road. We still have a long ways to go."

"I understand," said Jibby. "You take care now."

"You too, Jibby."

"Oh—and Ethan."

"Yes, Jibby?"

"Good luck with that dime machine."

ADVICE ON CHOOSING A DOG

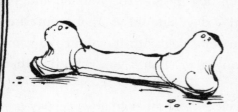 Like many of you out there, I love animals. So much, in fact, that I have had the words *I Love Animals* shaved into the side of my dog, Kevin. And at the cost of eighty-five cents per letter you can be assured that I am not kidding around.

Of the virtually hundreds of species of animals that populate this planet, may I say that dogs are far and away number one. I realize such an inflammatory statement is bound to result in an uproar from owners of cats, pigs, horses, or muskrats who will undoubtedly say, "Well, if dogs are so great, how come they are entirely unable to produce musk?"

This I cannot answer. But I do know that while your muskrat is doing the jitterbug out in muskratland, my dog is out fetching the newspaper, which is quite a trick considering I do not subscribe to the paper. Furthermore, after fetching the paper he can create an alibi for himself by playing dead.

Of course there are many other reasons for getting a dog besides the free newspaper angle. Dogs offer companionship, loyalty, and can help curb the burgeoning muskrat population.

But of the literally dozens of breeds available, how can you decide which dog is right for you? Should you get a big dog or a small dog? Should you get a purebred or a mix? Should you get a dog with the ability to warn you of impending danger, or should you get a dog that likes to chew?

Whichever you decide, remember to always spay or neuter your pets. And, if you can afford to, have it done professionally. The spaying and neutering of pets is a cause I truly believe in. It's certainly something worth writing about. And I know just where to write it. "Here, Kevin! Come here, boy!"

CHAPTER 12

Not more than thirty miles away from where Pinky stood at the side of the road growling suspiciously, a long black car was cruising down the highway. Inside the car, Mr. 29, Mr. 88, and Mr. 207 were involved in a spirited discussion while Mr. 5 sat silently in the front passenger seat with his arms folded and his clammy forehead glistening.

"Now what about smashing?" said Mr. 207. "How is that different than crushing?"

"I believe that smashing involves repeated blows with a heavy object," said Mr. 88. "Whereas crushing can be accomplished with just the mere weight of something."

"How about smooshing?" said Mr. 207. "How is smooshing different from smashing?"

"Smooshing is the grinding motion you make immediately after smashing," said Mr. 88. "Like when you smash a bug with your shoe. Afterward, you always give a bit of a smoosh by rotating your foot a few times to make sure. Any other questions?"

"I have a question," said Mr. 5, who had been riding in

silence for as long as he could stand it. "Are you all out of your minds? Who cares about squishing and smooshing and smashing? We have only one concern. To find Mr. Cheeseman and his three horrible little children. And we won't stop until we do. Is that understood?"

"Uh . . . actually," said Mr. 207, "I believe we'll have to stop before then. You see, we're almost out of gas."

Mr. 5 could only look to the sky, grit his teeth, shake his hands, and growl like an angry, frustrated wolverine with a sweaty, bald head.

The black car pulled off the rural highway and into a service station. The front doors opened and out came Mr. 5 and Mr. 207. The rear doors opened and out came Misters 29 and 88.

"Fill it up," said Mr. 5 to the other misters. "I'll be right back. This is the only gas station for miles. There's a good chance they stopped here as well."

The three men watched in silence as Mr. 5 walked into the small convenience store that also served as the office. No one spoke for a few moments until Mr. 207 broke the silence.

"What about mashing?"

"Same as smashing," said Mr. 88. "Except that mashing applies only to potatoes."

The two other men nodded as if to say "That makes perfect sense."

Inside the convenience store, the man behind the counter looked to be in his nineties, with thick glasses and, perched behind his left ear, a hearing aid so large it could probably pick up radio stations from Guam. He wore a threadbare pale blue cardigan that at one time had probably been bright blue.

Mr. 5 walked over and tossed a photo onto the counter. It was an old family photo of Mr. Cheeseman, Olivia, Jough, Maggie, and Gerard, all smiling for the camera.

"Have you seen these people?" Mr. 5 asked.

"Who wants to know?" the old man replied.

"Who wants to know?" said Mr. 5 sternly. "I do."

"Oh. Sorry. My eyesight's not what it used to be. I thought maybe it was that fella over there."

Mr. 5 was confused. He and the old man were the only people in the store. He looked in the direction of the old man's gaze.

"That is a magazine rack," Mr. 5 snapped.

"Oh. Well, like I told you, my eyesight's not so good these days. Hearing could use some improvement, too. Why, there was a time when I could hear a worm crawling through the dirt at fifty paces. Came in handy during the Depression when food was scarce. Now, back then, you could buy a car for fifty cents and still have enough left over for a—"

"Listen," Mr. 5 interrupted. "Have you seen these people or not?"

The old man picked up the photo and held it very close to his face.

"Ah, yes," he said with a smile. "Saw 'em just the other day."

"Which day, exactly?"

"Hmm, Tuesday I'd have to say. Tuesday and Wednesday."

"Tuesday *and* Wednesday?"

"Yup. Didn't see 'em Thursday. Had a doctor's appointment."

"So Wednesday was the last time you saw them?"

"I'd say so, yes."

"What time?"

"I believe it was six p.m. eastern, five p.m. central."

"Which way were they headed?"

The old man looked confused.

"Well, I don't really remember exactly," he said. "I suppose they were headed lots of different places throughout the course of the program. Bowling alley, rock quarry, back home again."

"Rock quarry? What are you talking about?" said Mr. 5, his patience exhausted.

"Why, the Flintstones of course," the old man said, looking at the photo and smiling once again. "They sure make me laugh. Fred's my favorite. Yabba dabba doo."

Mr. 5 reached out and angrily snatched the photo from the old man.

"Forget it," he snapped. "We'll just pay for the gas and be on our way."

"Very well," the old man said, leaning close to the pump readout. "Looks like it'll be $5,964. You know, back in the day you could fill your tank for a penny and still have enough left over for a pint of ice cream and a glass of Ovaltine."

"I think you're forgetting the decimal point."

"Huh?" the Old Man said, moving his face even closer to the readout. "Oh yes. Make that $59.64. That's quite a difference, isn't it?"

Mr. 5 handed the man sixty dollars in cash.

"Keep the change," he said, then strode out of the store in a huff.

"Well, that young lady was not very friendly at all, was she?" the old man said to the magazine rack.

When Mr. 5 returned to the car, the others were once again sitting inside.

"Gooshing is not an action," Mr. 88 was explaining. "It's a sound. Like when you step in a puddle and your socks get all wet—"

Mr. 88 stopped short when the door opened and Mr. 5 slithered in.

"Welcome back, sir," said Mr. 207. "Any luck?'

"Just shut up and drive," said Mr. 5.

"Which way?"

"My gut says they're heading west."

As the station wagon pulled back onto the highway, the sun was slowly sinking below the horizon like a leaky boat. Well, except for the fact that boats are not generally round, orange, and on fire. Hmm. Come to think of it, in no way whatsoever did the sun, in this instance, resemble a leaky boat. My apologies. That was a dreadful attempt at simile. Please allow me to try again.

As the station wagon pulled back onto the highway, the sun was slowly sinking below the horizon like a self-luminous, gaseous sphere comprised mainly of hydrogen and helium. Mr. Cheeseman and his family waved their last good-byes to Jibby, Three-Eyed Jake, Aristotle, Dizzy, Sammy, and Juanita.

When Jibby and his friends were no longer in sight, Mr. Cheeseman found Gerard in the rearview mirror.

"Gerard," he said. "I know you didn't mean to, but we must be very careful not to say anything to anyone about the LVR and its possible time travel capabilities. Is that understood?"

"Yes," said Gerard apologetically. "Don't worry. I won't do it again."

"You'd better not," said Jough. "It could ruin our chances of ever seeing Mom again." With that, Jough turned to his father.

"Dad?" he said. "Was Mom a good dancer?"

Mr. Cheeseman started to answer but stopped. He swallowed a lump in his throat, then tried again.

"Yes," he said. "She was a fabulous dancer. Absolutely fabulous."

Pinky growled again and Mr. Cheeseman drove faster.

Back at the roadside, Jibby and his crew of misfits loaded the chairs, the banquet tables, and everything else they had used to stage the shindig. When they finished, Jibby and Jake pulled Aristotle aside.

"So," began Jibby. "What do you think? Are they the ones?"

"They're the ones all right," said Aristotle, his molars working to soften the stiff pink bubble gum. "I remember them plain as day." Suddenly, his face lit up. "Did you hear that? I remember," he said. "Well, what do you know."

"So what do we do?" asked Jake. "Do we follow them?"

"I don't think that will be necessary," said Jibby. "If what Aristotle has predicted comes true, they'll find us. But just for now, maybe we should put Hollywood on hold."

Mr. Cheeseman and his family drove for what seemed like an eternity, especially to young Gerard, who, at his age, was prone to bouts of extreme fidgeting. After sitting for so long, he simply could not keep his legs and arms still.

"Ouch," said Maggie as one of Gerard's uncontrollable arms made contact with her kneecap. "Sit still, would you?"

"I can't help it," said Gerard. "I try and tell my arms and legs not to move but they just won't listen."

"I'm sorry," said Mr. Cheeseman. "I know you're all tired of being in the car. I was hoping to make it to the next town and get a motel, but we are officially in the middle of nowhere. It looks as though we're going to have to camp out."

"Yes!" Gerard exclaimed. "I love to camp out."

"Me too," said Steve.

Fifty miles away, a gray car pulled off the highway and into the same service station that Mr. 5 and his Plexiwave cohorts had just left moments before. In fact, the gas pump handle was still warm from Mr. 207's grip.

The doors to the gray car opened and out stepped Agents Aitch Dee and El Kyoo.

"Fill it up," said Aitch Dee to El Kyoo. "I'll be right back."

Aitch Dee walked into the convenience store and looked around to ensure that he and the elderly man behind the counter were the only two in the building.

"Have you seen this man?" he said, tossing a photograph of Ethan Cheeseman onto the counter.

"Who's askin'?" the old man demanded in his very old, very quavering voice.

"Abraham Lincoln," said Aitch Dee.

Upon hearing this, the old man didn't seem so old anymore. Even his voice suddenly sounded much younger when he removed his thick glasses and replied, "How goes the war, Mr. President?"

"I think we're going to march south and take them by surprise."

"I would suggest that west is the way to go."

"So he's been here?" asked Aitch Dee. "Ethan Cheeseman?"

"No," said the old man. "But another gentleman was here just moments ago asking the same question. They left here and headed west."

"Excellent. Good work, Agent Gee Doubleyou."

"Just doing my job," said Gee Doubleyou. "Would you like to buy a magazine?"

ADVICE ON DEALING WITH TRISKAIDEKAPHOBIA

What time is it when the clock strikes thirteen? If you said "Time to run for your lives!" then you may suffer from *triskaidekaphobia*, an abiding fear of the number thirteen. This is an affliction not to be taken lightly and help is available in the form of support groups, toll-free hotlines, and twelve-step programs. (There are some thirteen-step programs as well, but they are far less popular.)

These worthwhile organizations will assist you in coping with your fear of the number thirteen or, as triskaidekaphobia sufferers call it, fourteen. It is a common response to this phobia to simply pretend that the number does not exist. I first noticed this while traveling to Zurich for the annual International Conference on Unsolicited Advice. As I boarded the airplane, I noticed that it had no thirteenth row. They left it out.

It's a bit disconcerting to realize you are flying with an airline that is superstitious. I could only hope that a black cat did not cross our flight path.

Triskaidekaphobia is certainly nothing to laugh about. But what is to be done about this completely irrational fear shared by an estimated "fourteen" million people? The best advice I can give you at this time is to follow your first instinct and, when you encounter that dreaded number, *run for your lives*!

CHAPTER ~~13~~ 14

When you're on the run from secret government agencies, international superspies, and evil, murderous corporate villains, it's not always possible to get to a hotel, making it necessary, on occasion, to camp out. As a result, Mr. Cheeseman and his family always traveled with two tents, four sleeping bags, a gas stove, a lantern, and two prefab fire logs.

As the station wagon pulled off the main road, the moon hung in the sky like a rotating, reflective orb with an approximate diameter of 2,158 miles. Mr. Cheeseman drove down a dirt road for a short time before before turning onto an even smaller, bumpier dirt road. After a few minutes, he pulled the station wagon to the side of the road and turned off the engine.

"This looks like a good place to camp for the night," he said.

"Are you sure, Dad?" said Jough.

"It's just an open field. We won't be bothering anyone and no one should bother us way out here."

"But what about the time we camped out in that city park?" said Gerard.

"Yes," said Maggie. "And the next morning we woke up on a golf course."

"You don't have to remind me of that," said Mr. Cheeseman. "I've still got a golf ball–sized dent on the back of my head. But there's no confusing this place with a golf course, that's for sure."

Mr. Cheeseman and his children piled out of the car and immediately began setting up the two tents, which was always easier to do during daylight hours. To make the job less difficult, Mr. Cheeseman turned on the car's headlights, being very careful not to use the high beams.

"Can we build a fire?" asked Gerard as he pounded in the last tent stake. "And roast marshmallows?"

In addition to the two tents, four sleeping bags, the gas stove, the lantern, and the prefab fire logs, Mr. Cheeseman's family always traveled with at least one large bag of marshmallows, just in case. It was one of the few fun things about being on the run.

"I don't see why not," said Mr. Cheeseman, who could eat half a bag of roasted marshmallows all on his own.

While Jough and Mr. Cheeseman gathered several large rocks to make a fire pit, Maggie and Gerard began scouring the area for long pointy sticks.

"Don't wander off now, Gerard," Maggie said. "There might be wild animals out here."

"We're not afraid of wild animals. Are we, Steve?"

"Not us," Steve agreed.

Maggie couldn't resist and tossed a rock through the darkness into the nearby weeds. She laughed as Gerard and Steve screamed and ran back to the camp, leaving her to find suitably pointy sticks on her own.

"Mmm, that one was perfect," said Mr. Cheeseman, eating his tenth marshmallow directly from the stick. "We really should do this more often."

"If I could," said Gerard, "I would camp out every day for the rest of my life."

"And how would you wash your hair?" asked Maggie.

"I wouldn't," said Gerard.

"Disgusting," said Maggie.

It was at that precise moment Mr. Cheeseman realized he and his children were not alone in the wide-open field.

"Excuse me," came a deep and deliberate voice from the darkness.

Mr. Cheeseman jumped to his feet. Maggie screamed. Gerard wheeled around, causing his marshmallow to fly off its stick and land in Maggie's hair, which caused Maggie to scream again. Pinky sprang into action, growling out into the darkness while hiding behind Mr. Cheeseman.

"Sorry. Didn't mean to scare ya'll," said the owner of the deep voice as he stepped out of the darkness and into the orangey firelight. "My name's Clancy. Clancy Finkleman."

Clancy was a solid-looking man with a square jaw and eyes in a constant state of squintiness. Not the kind of squintiness that comes from having poor vision or from having the sun in one's eyes, but the kind that comes from being in constant pain. He wore a red plaid shirt, jeans, and a leather cowboy hat and had a knapsack slung over his left shoulder.

"You scared the dickens out of us," said Mr. Cheeseman. "We thought we were all alone out here."

"Heck, I thought the same thing," said Clancy. "But I was driving by and I seen the light from your campfire and decided I'd see who else was crazy enough to be way out here in the middle of nowheres."

"You can see our fire from the road?" asked Mr. Cheeseman, with no small amount of concern.

"Well, I wasn't exactly driving on the road. You see, I like to take me a shortcut or two whenever possible. I know this country like the back of my hand, and my trusty pickup truck will go just about anywheres I tell her to."

"Well, why don't you sit down and take a load off," said Mr. Cheeseman, who would normally be suspicious of strangers except for the fact that Pinky, once she got over her initial scare, did not growl any further. In fact, she walked right over and began sniffing at the dull, dusty points of Clancy's cowboy boots.

"Would you like a marshmallow?" asked Jough. "They're really good."

"And sticky," said Maggie pointedly as she tried her best to remove the toasted goo from her hair.

"I ain't got much of a sweet tooth," said Clancy. "But I'd be happier than a worm on a wet sidewalk if I could sit and visit for a spell. I haven't talked to another human being in pert near three days now."

Clancy lowered himself onto a rock next to the fire with a pained groan.

"You look like a cowboy," Gerard blurted out in his best blurting voice.

Clancy chuckled. "That might be because I am. Been cowboyin' durn near all my life."

"I want to be a cowboy when I grow up," said Gerard.

"You want to be everything when you grow up," said Maggie.

"I think I'd make a great cowboy," Gerard said in self-defense. "I can talk to cows, you know."

"I hardly think yelling the word *moo* to a herd of cows while traveling at sixty miles per hour is quite the same thing," said Maggie.

"Are those your cows we passed a ways back, Mr. Finkle-man?" asked Jough.

"Nope. 'Fraid not. I don't own no cattle. In fact, just about everything I got to my name is on my person as we speak."

"Just like us," said Gerard. "Everything we own is on top of our car."

Clancy looked at the top-heavy station wagon and nodded ever so slightly.

"Yup," he said. "You folks got the right idea, that's for sure. A man gets too much stuff, he spends half his time just trying to keep track of it all."

"Clancy Finkleman. That doesn't sound like a cowboy name to me," Gerard blurted again.

Maggie thought of backhanding her little brother but decided instead that she fully agreed with him. Clancy Finkleman did not sound like a cowboy name.

"Yup," exhaled Clancy as he removed his hat and placed it on his knee. "That might be part of my problem. You see, I'm on my way to Montana. For the annual cowboy poetry contest. I enter every year."

"Have you ever won?" asked Jough.

"Nope," Clancy said sadly. "I keep tryin' though. I reckon I've written some pretty good poems this past year, but you never know."

"I'd love to hear one," said Maggie.

"Well, okay, you twisted my arm." Clancy pulled a small, well-creased notebook from his back pocket. "But I want your honest opinion. Don't go sayin' you like it iffen you don't."

"We'll be brutally honest," said Jough.

"Well," said Mr. Cheeseman while chewing on his eleventh marshmallow, "I think being just plain honest is good enough. Let's leave out the brutality, shall we?"

"I appreciate that," said Clancy. "My hide may be tough as leather, but the heart of a poet can be soft as that marshmallow you're gnawin' on."

He flipped through the notebook, looking for the perfect poem for his audience.

"Ah, here we go," he said. He cleared his throat and began to read. "The sun falls from the sky like a big cow pie / and the lone wolf bays at the moon. / I take off my chaps and get ready to nap / as my saddle sores swell like balloons."

Clancy looked up from his notebook hopefully. Mr. Cheeseman and his children sat stiffly, wishing they hadn't agreed to absolute candor. Their faces registered the exact look you would expect from anyone who had just listened to a poem about chafing.

"Well?" said Clancy. "You hated it, didn't you?"

"It's not that we hated it," began Maggie.

"I hated it," said Steve, which caused Maggie to deliver a backhand smack to Gerard's chest.

"What?" Gerard protested. "I didn't say anything."

"Please excuse my little brother," said Maggie. "But I believe what he's trying to say is that the poem is a little bit—how shall I say—rhymey."

"Rhymey?" said Clancy.

"Yes. It all rhymes very nicely but it doesn't give me much of a sense of what it's really like to be a cowboy."

Clancy exhaled heavily and looked at the ground and the children immediately felt that perhaps honesty is not always the best policy.

"But that's only one poem," said Jough. "Maybe you could read another one."

"Naw," said Clancy. "They're all pretty much the same, I reckon. Some are even rhymier than that one. I'm afraid I'm just not a very good poet."

"Well, I'm sure you're a very good cowboy," said Maggie.

"I reckon I am. Truth is, though, a fella can only cowboy

for so long before he starts to feel like a stray dog; long in the tooth and short on patience for the cold, hard ground on which he sleeps, thankful to be above it for now and not below. Like that old dog, desperate for nourishment of body and soul, the cowboy longs for a knife that can carve away a lonely night. Most times, that knife is a song, sung out low and slow to stars long since dead and calling you to join 'em. That thought is there for a moment, but those stars will have to wait. There's just too darned much work to do."

Clancy looked up and noticed that Ethan and the kids, even Steve the sock puppet, had been hanging on his every word.

"Wow," said Jough. "That was great."

"And you said you weren't a very good poet," said Gerard.

"Aw, that weren't a poem," said Clancy. "That was just talkin'."

"But it was a poem," said Maggie. "A beautiful poem. About what it's really like to be a cowboy."

"And it wasn't rhymey at all," said Gerard.

"You really liked it?" asked Clancy, his posture improving immediately.

"It was very compelling," said Mr. Cheeseman.

"And very truthful," said Maggie.

"I don't think I want to be a cowboy when I grow up," said Gerard. "Now I want to be a poet."

"You want to be a poet?" said Maggie, entirely unconvinced.

"Why not?" said Gerard. "I know lots of poems. Listen to this one. 'Beans, beans, the magical fruit—' "

"Okay, Gerard," said Mr. Cheeseman. "That'll do just fine."

"It's just as well," said Jough. "That one is pretty rhymey, if I remember."

"So you think I should write some poems that aren't so rhymey?" asked Clancy.

"Just write the truth as you know it," said Maggie.

Clancy rubbed his chin and thought for a moment. "Okay. I reckon maybe I'll take your advice on this one. You know, all of a sudden I feel like maybe I finally know what the heck I'm doing. Like I can finally write the kind of poems these contest judges are looking for. Now if I could just do something about my name."

"Well, that shouldn't be a problem," said Jough.

"Yeah," said Gerard. "We change our names all the time."

Jough and Maggie each shot Gerard a dirty look.

"He means that we sometimes make up different names for ourselves just for fun," Jough covered.

"I think we should take turns coming up with a good cowboy name for Clancy," said Maggie.

"I'll go first," Gerard volunteered. "Okay, let's see. Instead of Clancy Finkleman, I think your new cowboy name should be . . . Wild Bill Finkleman."

For a moment there was silence.

"Well?" asked Gerard. "What do you think?"

"Should I be brutally honest or just honest?" asked Clancy.

"Just honest, please," said Gerard.

"Well, I don't think it quite does the trick. But it was a heck of a nice try."

"I've got one," said Maggie. "How about . . . Tex Roper?"

Clancy nodded slowly. "It's not bad. Got a nice ring to it. But I'm not from Texas. I'm from Mississippi."

"Then how about Miss Roper?" squeaked Steve.

"Don't be ridiculous," said Maggie with absolutely no tolerance in her voice.

"Okay, my turn," said Jough. "I think you should change your name to . . . Buck Weston."

"Ahh," said Maggie angrily as she kicked at the dirt.

"What?" said Jough. "You don't like it?"

"Of course I like it. It's perfect. You always think of the best names."

"It is pretty durn good," said Clancy. He tried it on for size by repeating the name several times more. "Buck Weston. It's got a good ring to it. Okay then. From now on, my official cowboy name will be Buck Weston."

"With your new name and your new style of poetry, I think you've got a pretty good chance of winning," said Jough.

"If I do, it'll be all because of you folks. I don't know quite how to thank ya'll."

"You can mention us in your acceptance speech," said Jough.

"I sure will," said Buck. "But right now, before I get goin', I'd like to give ya'll somethin' to remember me by. Hold on."

Mr. Cheeseman and the children watched as Buck stood up and walked off into the darkness in the direction he had come.

"What do you think, Dad?" said Jough. "He seems like a nice enough guy."

"As long as Pinky likes him we're okay."

A few moments later, Buck returned and sat down on the rock once more. He didn't seem to have anything more than when he had left, but his right hand was closed tightly. He opened it to reveal three beautifully crafted Native American arrowheads.

"Wow," said Maggie, the archer in her coming alive. "Are those . . . ?"

"They sure are. I've found quite a few of 'em over the years. I'd like each of you to have one."

"This is a fabulous gift, Mr. Weston," said Maggie, taking a small reddish brown arrowhead. "I've studied archery for years but I've never held a real handmade arrowhead before. It's going to be my personal good-luck charm."

"Me too," said Gerard.

"That's awfully nice of you, Buck," said Mr. Cheeseman. "I think we should give you something in return. A good-luck charm for the contest."

Mr. Cheeseman walked to the car, opened the back, and unzipped a dark green duffel bag. He returned holding a red necktie. On the necktie the letter *U* had been stitched hundreds of times in bright yellow thread.

"This is my lucky necktie. I've had it since college. I know it's not much to look at and I wouldn't expect you to wear it, but if you keep it with you, maybe it'll bring you the same kind of luck it's brought me over the years. The letter *U* is the symbol for uranium, which I've always found to be one of the luckier elements."

"That is mighty nice of you, Mr. Cheeseman. I'll take all the luck I can get these days. You know, you folks have been awfully kind and I sure would like to stay and get to know you better, but I really should hit the road. I've got a lot of poems to write between here and Montana."

Ethan and the children said their good-byes to yet another friend they were all but certain they would never see again.

They climbed into the tents, into their sleeping bags, and fell asleep with their bellies full of marshmallows and good-luck charms beneath their pillows.

CHAPTER 15

The only problem with driving through the middle of nowhere with Agent El Kyoo at your side is that he just happened to be a notorious backseat driver, a problem exacerbated by the fact that he did all of his backseat driving from the front seat. And though the benefits of unsolicited advice are too numerous to name, I would like to go on record as saying that it should never be given to someone who is behind the wheel of a car, as it is quite possible it will result in advanced levels of irritation and, in extreme cases, punching. And, as Aitch Dee navigated the gray car down the tortuous highway, El Kyoo's driving hints were beginning to drive him absolutely crazy.

"Watch for ice," said El Kyoo, reading the road sign as they whizzed by it.

"It's June," said Aitch Dee. "I doubt we'll be encountering any ice."

"Sorry. Just trying to be helpful." Ten minutes of silence passed before El Kyoo spoke up again. "Sharp turn ahead."

"I can read," said Aitch Dee, an almost audible strain in

his otherwise expressionless voice. "Now, I would appreciate it if you would please keep quiet and let me concentrate on the road."

"Sure, no problem. By the way, how do we know we're going the right way?"

"We don't. We're working on our best assumption based on the intelligence gathered from satellite surveillance. Plus, there have been several reported sightings of them in this area."

"I see. Watch out for livestock," said El Kyoo, pointing to another road sign.

"All right, that's it," said Aitch Dee, his voice finding a new register for the first time since going to work for the top secret government agency.

"You're in violation of Section 18 Jay regarding emotional outbursts," said El Kyoo. "Just so you know."

"I don't care," said Aitch Dee in a singsongy voice. "I'm sick and tired of your backseat driving. I don't need you to tell me to watch out for ice, sharp turns, livestock, or the queen of England, okay? It's June seventeenth, it's seventy-two degrees in the shade, and I doubt very much that a cow is suddenly going to sprint out in front of the—"

"Livestock," said El Kyoo, pointing dead ahead, his eyes wide as saucers.

"What did I just say?" said Aitch Dee. "I don't need you to—"

With that, El Kyoo forgot all about Section 18 Jay and let out a very emotional scream, his eyes increasing in size from that of mere saucers to full-sized dinner plates.

Aitch Dee looked back to the road to see, standing directly in the middle of it, a very large and very sturdy-looking Tibetan yak. Aitch Dee stomped hard on the brake pedal and the car skidded toward the yak, which just looked at the car with a face that seemed to say "Huh?"

With the sound of crunching metal, the car struck the yak. The stunned animal rolled up onto the hood and against the windshield. A shower of broken glass rained down on Aitch Dee and El Kyoo as the yak continued rolling up over the roof of the car with a thunderous crunch. It fell to the pavement with a thud as the car went into a violent spin, making several complete rotations, finally coming to stop on the side of the road amid a cloud of dust.

"What happened?" said Aitch Dee, when he finally regained his breath.

"I think . . . ," said El Kyoo, panting heavily. "I think we hit a cow."

"That was no cow," said Aitch Dee.

"Then what was it?"

"I'm not sure. It looked like a bull with long hair."

Aitch Dee opened his door, letting in no small amount of dust. He barked out a cough and climbed out to assess the damage to the car while El Kyoo walked back to assess the damage to the yak, which was lying motionless against a road sign. The sign read *Watch for Falling Rock*.

The front end of the car was badly damaged. The headlights were smashed and steam poured out from beneath the dented hood. Aitch Dee tried to open the hood but it was too badly mangled.

"It won't open," said Aitch Dee as he looked back to see El Kyoo carrying a very large rock toward the yak.

"What are you doing?"

"I'm making it look like an accident," said El Kyoo in a steady tone.

"It *was* an accident," said Aitch Dee. "Now put that rock down and give me a hand with the hood."

El Kyoo sighed and set the rock on top of the yak, then walked back toward the car. As he did, Aitch Dee went white and pointed in El Kyoo's direction.

"Bull," is all he could manage.

"It's a bull, I get it," said El Kyoo. "You don't have to rub it in. And if you keep insisting on violating Section—"

"No, I mean . . . *run!*"

El Kyoo spun around to see that not only was the yak not dead, it was also not very happy at having been struck by a speeding car and then having a rock dropped on top of it. It was standing and snorting loudly, its narrow eyes trained on El Kyoo's soft, bowling-pin-shaped body.

"Easy now," said El Kyoo in as soothing a voice as one can make without the use of inflection. "No reason to get excited here."

The yak wholeheartedly disagreed and charged. El Kyoo spun on his heel and ran back toward the car with the highly agitated yak right on his heels.

"Don't run this way!" yelled Aitch Dee.

The yak chased Aitch Dee and El Kyoo around the car, lap after lap, kicking up dust and getting so close that El

Kyoo swore he could feel the animal's breath on his tender backside.

"It's no use," panted El Kyoo. "I'm too out of shape. I can't run anymore."

"I don't think we've got much of a choice here."

It would be only a matter of seconds before the two men, completely out of breath, were gouged by the yak's pointy conical horns. They had three choices as Aitch Dee saw it. The first was to stop running and try to reason with the yak.

"Excuse me, but please accept our sincerest apologies for running you over with our car. Allow us to present you with this coupon for a free bale of hay as compensation for your troubles." Not likely.

The second choice they had was to fall to the ground and roll beneath the car, which is a viable option if you are shaped like a kite but not if you are shaped like a bowling pin. The third possible course of action was to climb on top of the car, out of reach of the yak.

"Follow me," yelled Aitch Dee as he dove onto the hood and then climbed up to the car's dented roof. El Kyoo leaped onto the hood as well, just as the yak took a swipe, tearing out the seat of his gray pants.

"That was close," said El Kyoo as he joined Aitch Dee on the roof. "But he's ruined my pants."

"You're lucky that's all he ruined. Nice baby blue underwear, by the way."

"They were a gift," said El Kyoo. "From my mother."

"That's weird," said Aitch Dee.

Having the agents out of reach did not make the yak very happy. In fact, it only frustrated it to the point of repeatedly ramming the side of the already dented gray car.

Blam! Blam! Blam!

El Kyoo and Aitch Dee held each other tightly as the yak ran its horns into the car over and over, hoping to knock the agents from the safety of their perch.

"Do something!" yelled Aitch Dee. "He's destroying the car."

"Do what?" said El Kyoo calmly.

"I don't know, shoot him!"

"I refuse to shoot a defenseless animal."

"Does he look defenseless to you?" said Aitch Dee.

"Look," said El Kyoo, pointing down the highway in the direction they had come. "A car. They can help us."

The two men waved their hands above their heads and yelled at the top of their lungs, as if the sight of a Tibetan yak ramming the side of a car wouldn't be enough to get someone's attention.

"Hey," Aitch Dee yelled. "Stop! Help!"

But the little brown car did not stop. It only slowed down briefly as the driver honked the horn and stuck his head out the window.

"Hey, fellows. Do not have a cow!"

Pavel cackled uncontrollably as Leon took time out from feeding his beloved fish to stick his head out the other window and call out in his best yak impression, "They said terrible things about your mother!"

The yak, not happy to hear this, continued its assault on the car with renewed vigor as Aitch Dee and El Kyoo watched the little brown car disappear around the bend.

"I hate that guy," said Aitch Dee.

The yak continued to batter one side of the car until it looked as though it had taken last place in a demolition derby. When its shape resembled that of a boomerang, the yak finally stopped, turned, and lumbered into the pasture across the road.

CHAPTER 16

"Do we have to camp out again tonight?" asked Maggie as the station wagon rattled down the highway, slightly to the left of the middle of nowhere. "I'd like a chance to wash my hair and to sleep in a real bed."

"Okay," said Mr. Cheeseman. "But I'm afraid that might mean a little extra time in the car." Mr. Cheeseman and his family had been driving all day and Gerard's arms and legs were becoming more and more fidgety. Even Jough had had just about enough.

"I think I'd rather camp out again than have to ride in this car anymore."

"I know and I'm sorry," said Mr. Cheeseman, sensing he might soon have a mutiny on his hands. "Just hang in there a little longer. There's a town coming up in about an hour. We'll find a motel and spend the night there."

"Sounds great," said Jough. "But are you sure it's safe?"

"Pinky hasn't growled in more than a day," said Mr. Cheeseman. "Looks like we gave 'em the slip."

As the next hour dragged by, Maggie and Gerard passed the time by reading the license plates of other cars that whizzed by.

It should be noted that much can be learned by reading license plate slogans. For instance, you will learn that Arizona is the "Grand Canyon State," which means that somewhere in Arizona there is a really large hole in the ground. Idaho, on the other hand, is the land of "Famous Potatoes," which means there are a lot of little holes in the ground from which potatoes have been removed. And Minnesota is the "Land of Ten Thousand Lakes," which suggests there are approximately that many holes in the ground all filled with water.

Yes, you can learn a great deal by reading license plate slogans, but when you've been in the car all day and on the run from secret government agencies, international superspies, and evil weapons manufacturers for nearly two years, it can also become quite tedious.

Because of this, Mr. Cheeseman and his children were nothing short of delighted when finally they found themselves driving through the center of a smallish town with mostly smallish houses and quaint little shops, all closed up for the night.

Other than this rather vague description, there's little else I can tell you about the town. Not because there isn't more to tell, but because any further details might give away the town's location. For the safety of Mr. Cheeseman and his family, the name of the town and its precise location must remain a secret, should this text fall into the wrong hands. What I will tell you is that the town was located somewhere in the western or eastern United States.

"This looks like a nice little town," said Maggie. "Maybe we could make this our new home."

"I don't see why not," said Mr. Cheeseman. "We'll stay the night and see how things look in the morning."

"That looks like it might be a good place to stay right there," said Jough, pointing up ahead to a two-story white house with green shutters. It had a large front porch with a white porch swing and a wooden sign hanging above the door that read *Coral's Bed-and-Breakfast.*

"Sure, let's give it a try," said Mr. Cheeseman, pulling the station wagon into the crunchy gravel driveway.

"Okay, you kids wait here. If you see anyone suspicious, honk the horn and I'll come running. Meanwhile, I'll see if they can accommodate us," said Mr. Cheeseman. He climbed out of the car, walked to the front door, and knocked. While he waited, he watched in amusement as several moths repeatedly ran headlong into the porch light. He wondered what they could possibly be thinking.

I happen to know exactly what they were thinking and it was this: "Wheeeeee! Ouch! Wheeeeee! Ouch! Wheeeeee!" And so on.

No one answered, so Mr. Cheeseman again moved his knuckles toward the heavy wooden door of the large white house. Before they could connect the door opened, revealing an extremely plump woman in a shapeless pink dress with pale yellow flowers. She was sitting on a four-wheeled electric scooter. She unlatched the door, then backed the scooter up to make room for the door to open inward.

"Good evening," said the woman. "Sorry to take so long to answer. I was in the study, watching the news. You know they captured two Bengal tigers at a miniature golf course in Utah?"

"You don't say," said Mr. Cheeseman.

"They wouldn't report it if it wasn't true. Luckily no one was hurt. Anyway, I'm Coral Bjornsen and this is my bed-and-breakfast. What can I do for you?"

"Well, my children and I were just passing through town and saw your place. We thought we might like to stay here for a day or two. We'll be needing two adjoining rooms if you've got them."

"I sure do," said Coral. "In fact, the whole place is empty right this minute. Come on in and let's get you registered."

Coral backed the scooter up and slammed into the wall behind her, which had already been marred by several tire marks.

"Oh, freckles!" she said. "I'm still trying to get used to this crazy thing. I got it a couple of weeks ago after I had surgery."

"I'm sorry to hear that," said Mr. Cheeseman, following Coral's scooter down the hallway toward the office. "Everything okay?"

"Oh yes. Just my lower left wisdom tooth. Impacted, it was. Hopefully I'll be back on my feet in a month or so."

Coral's scooter collided with the wall on the way into the tiny office.

"Oh, bananas!" She backed up, straightened out, and drove into the office and over to the desk. Mr. Cheeseman straightened a picture on the wall before following her inside.

"Okay," she said, opening the registration book. "Please have a seat while we get some information from you. Let's start with your name."

"Uh . . . Fred," Mr. Cheeseman lied as he sat down in the small wooden chair across from Coral. "Fred . . . Stapler."

Mr. Cheeseman tried hard not to look directly at the staple gun resting on Coral's desk.

"Okay, Mr. Stapler. What's your home address?"

"Home address?" said Mr. Cheeseman, who had never been very good at lying.

"Yes. I need a home address or I can't rent you a room. It's a very strict policy I'm afraid."

"Yes, I understand," said Mr. Cheeseman. "My home address is . . . 123 Main Street . . . New York, New York . . . 54321."

Mr. Cheeseman watched in amazement as Coral jotted down the address without batting an eye—or any other body part, for that matter.

"Home phone?"

"Yes, it's, uh . . . 555-HOME."

"Well, that's pretty handy, isn't it? Work phone?"

"It's, uh . . . 555-WORK."

"Well, you must know someone at the phone company."

"Yes. My sister . . . Stacy."

"Stacy Stapler?"

"Yes, that's it," Mr. Cheeseman lied once more.

Lying is never a good thing to do, but when you're being hunted by evil people wishing to do you harm, it sometimes becomes necessary.

"Okay then," said Coral. "Here are the keys to rooms four and five. They're right down the hall on the left. Breakfast is served at eight o'clock. And we do have a strict no pets policy."

"Well, that won't be a problem. We don't have any pets."

"Good, because I am very allergic to dog and cat hair. As well as red peppers. But only if I eat them. The peppers, that is, not the dogs and cats. Which is not to say that I eat dogs and cats. I only meant that I could eat them without an allergic reaction. I mean, as far as I know, having never eaten one. But of course I never would. I mean, perhaps if I were stranded on a desert island and that's all there was, then—"

"We'll be paying cash," said Mr. Cheeseman.

"Right," said Coral.

As Mr. Cheeseman and the children settled in for the night, they found the rooms at the bed-and-breakfast to be small but very comfortable. In one room, there was a queen-size bed for Jough and Mr. Cheeseman as well as a daybed by the window, just long enough to fit Gerard's short, fidgety body. The connecting room was smaller, with one twin bed for Maggie alone.

"It's not fair," said Gerard. "Why should she get her own room?"

"Yes, it's not fair," Steve agreed. "We want to have our own room."

"You don't need your own room, Steve. And neither do you, Gerard," said Mr. Cheeseman, in no mood to argue. "Maggie is a girl and she needs her privacy. You'll understand when you get older. Now let's get our teeth brushed and get off to sleep."

"Dad, what about Pinky?" Jough asked.

"She'll be fine in the car."

"But what if she senses danger? How will she be able to warn us?"

"I don't know. They do have a strict no pets policy here. Coral, the owner, is very allergic to animal hair."

"But Dad," said Gerard. "Pinky has no hair, remember?"

"Hmm. You're right," said Mr. Cheeseman.

At roughly that same time, no more than forty miles away, in a similarly quiet town with similarly smallish houses and quaint shops, Aitch Dee and El Kyoo walked in from the highway, their feet swollen and sore and El Kyoo's stomach growling angrily.

"Well, we made it," said Aitch Dee. "We made it back to civilization."

"My feet are numb," said El Kyoo.

"I wish mine were numb. That would be an improvement over what they actually are. Now let's find a place to stay. Tomorrow we can rent a car and get back on the trail of Mr. Cheeseman and that device of his."

"I need food," said El Kyoo. "I'm so hungry I could eat dirt."

"You may have to eat dirt. This whole town seems to be closed down for the night."

"Not quite," said El Kyoo, pointing up ahead. "The lights are still on at that burger joint."

The two hungry, weary men trudged down the small town's main street toward the well-lit burger joint, a 1950s-style restaurant called Earl T's Burger Barn. They were surprised to find the door locked and the place empty except for a young man in a paper hat, mopping the floor.

"Sorry," said the young man, who stopped mopping long enough to yell loudly through the glass. "We close at eleven. Only the drive-through is open now."

Aitch Dee and El Kyoo circled around the restaurant until they came to the drive-through. Aitch Dee tapped on the window and a few seconds later, a well-freckled young woman slid the window open.

"Hi, welcome to Earl T's," she said with confusion. "May I . . . help you?"

"Four double cheeseburgers, two orders of fries, a strawberry shake, and a chocolate shake," said El Kyoo.

"And a salad for me," said Aitch Dee.

"I'm sorry," said the young woman. "But I can't take your order."

"What?" said El Kyoo, the panic in his voice almost detectable by the naked ear. "What do mean you can't take our order?"

"You have to have a car to use the drive-through."

"We have a car," El Kyoo protested, his voice beginning to tremble. "We just don't have it with us at the moment. It broke down out on the highway and we're starving. Can't you make an exception this once?"

"I'm sorry. It's company policy. I could lose my job."

"Is there any other place open in town?" asked El Kyoo hopefully.

"I'm afraid not."

Before closing the window and locking it, the young woman managed to tell both El Kyoo and Aitch Dee to have a nice day, which was strange considering that it was almost midnight and the odds that this day could somehow turn out to be a nice one in the five or so remaining minutes seemed slim at best.

"Well, that's it," said Aitch Dee. "We'll just have to eat in the morning. Right now let's . . . what are you doing?"

El Kyoo was standing just to the side of the drive-through lane with his right thumb extended upward.

"She didn't say we had to *own* a car to use the drive-through," he said.

"You're going to hitchhike through the drive-through?"

"I told you, I'm starving," snapped El Kyoo.

"You know you're in violation of Section 18 Jay?"

"Can we just forget about that stupid section?" said El Kyoo, years of emotion rising to the surface. "It's a stupid rule anyway!"

"Well," said Aitch Dee. "Okay. I won't report you if you don't report me."

Before El Kyoo could agree, he spotted a long black car with tinted windows driving slowly toward them.

"Look! I knew someone would come along." El Kyoo smiled and tried to look as friendly as possible but the car did not stop for them and proceeded on to the order window. The four men in the black car hadn't even noticed the hungry government agents, as three of them were engaged in a meaningful discussion about the subtle differences between crunching and munching while the fourth man turned up the radio to try and drown them out.

"Well?" said Aitch Dee as the car drove past. "Now what?"

"We wait," said El Kyoo. "The next car is bound to give us a ride."

"We walked twelve miles through the middle of nowhere and not one person stopped to pick us up thanks to you and your baby blue underwear sticking out of your pants. So what makes you think someone's going to help us out now?"

"Because I am an optimist," said El Kyoo. "Whereas you see the glass as half empty, I like to look at it as half full. See? Look here."

Aitch Dee looked up to see a rusted blue pickup truck making its way toward them. The truck slowed to a stop and the driver, a solid-looking man with squinty eyes and a leather cowboy hat, leaned across to the passenger side window.

"Where you fellas headed?" said Buck Weston to the two stranded agents.

"Just to the end of the drive-through," said El Kyoo, pointing over his shoulder with his hitchhiking thumb.

"I'm headin' that way myself," said Buck. "Hop in."

The two agents climbed into the dusty truck, trying to avoid sitting on the springs that had begun to come through the overworn seat.

"We really appreciate this," said El Kyoo. "You know they won't let you order if you don't have a car?"

"Is that a fact? Doesn't seem right, does it?"

As Buck drove toward the order window, Aitch Dee noticed something hanging from the rearview mirror. Something very interesting.

"That's quite a unique necktie you've got there. Mind if I ask where you got it?"

"Not at all," said Buck. "Got it from my good friends Ethan, Jough, Maggie, and Gerard. It's my new good-luck charm."

"Really," said Aitch Dee. "I'd love to hear more about these good friends of yours."

As Buck leaned in toward the window to give the young woman his order, Aitch Dee reached into his breast pocket and removed the photo of Ethan Cheeseman, which pictured the brilliant physicist dressed in a white shirt and a red *U*-covered tie.

SOME GENEROUS ADVICE ON GIFT GIVING

All gifts are not created equal. Historically speaking, there are good gifts and there are bad gifts.

Good gifts: A bottle of champagne, a box of fine Belgian chocolates, the Statue of Liberty.

Bad gifts: A bottle of shampoo, a box of fine Belgian matches, the Trojan Horse.

Of all the annual gift-giving occasions, none is more expensive than Christmas.

One way I've found to cut back on my yuletide gift spending is by adopting a little holiday tradition known as the Secret Santa. Here's how it works. Rather than buy a gift for each and every member of your family, you simply drop your names into a hat, then fake your own deaths and move to Brazil.

A less extreme version involves drawing a name from the hat and buying a gift for that person. To make things more interesting, the name you draw is kept a secret. To make things even more interesting, the hat is filled with fierce, biting ants.

Keeping the name a secret, though it adds an

element of mystery to the process, prevents you from asking that person what type of gift he or she would prefer, ensuring that you will find yourself wandering through the mall in a stupor until they turn off the escalator.

For this reason I advise that, before dropping the names into the ant-infested hat, each person should loudly state their name and what they would like for Christmas. As in, "My name is Carl and I would like a new hat."

So, be it a new hat, a box of matches, or a giant wooden horse full of bloodthirsty Trojans, the thing you should remember above all else when giving someone a gift is to make certain that you are not giving him something that might provide nosy government agents with information as to your whereabouts.

CHAPTER 17

It was just after midnight. Mr. Cheeseman and his two sons slept soundly in their cozy room at the bed-and-breakfast while Pinky, recently smuggled in, snored softly, curled up on a rug at the foot of the bed.

In the adjacent room, Maggie was having a much harder time finding sleep. She lay on her back practicing the breathing exercises her mother had taught her but ultimately was unable to lose consciousness. Suddenly, she could hear something in the room that was not the sound of her own breathing. She opened her eyes and before her loomed something that caused her to lose her breath altogether. It was a woman. A strange-looking woman, roller-skating back and forth at the foot of Maggie's bed.

"Who are you?" Maggie demanded. "What do you want?"

The woman turned to Maggie and said nothing for a moment, then finally spoke.

"Fraud, fraud, it's not the dog," she moaned.

"Fraud, fraud, it's not the dog? What do you mean it's not the dog?" Maggie said sternly.

She received no answer from the woman, who repeated her message twice more, then smiled calmly, skated through the wall, and disappeared.

Mr. Cheeseman and the boys were dead to the world when suddenly the quiet disappeared with a loud pounding on the door that separated the two rooms.

"Open the door!" yelled Maggie. "It's stuck! Hurry!"

Mr. Cheeseman flew out of bed and ran to the door. The only problem was, the room was dark and utterly unfamiliar to him and finding the door was not easy. He tripped over Pinky, who let out a yelp. On his hands and knees, he crawled toward the sound of Maggie's voice, which was getting louder with each passing second.

"Help! Open the door!"

Finally, Mr. Cheeseman was able to open the door and in ran Maggie, crying and out of breath.

"What is it?" Mr. Cheeseman said, taking the trembling girl into his arms. "What's wrong?"

"A woman was in my room," said Maggie. "She's gone now. But I saw her. She was right there at the foot of my bed."

"Are you sure?" asked Mr. Cheeseman.

"Yes, I'm sure. She spoke to me. She said 'Fraud, fraud, it's not the dog.' "

"Now what do you think she meant by that?"

"I don't know. I asked her but she just skated right through the wall."

"Skated through the wall?"

"What's going on, Dad?" Jough yawned.

"Yeah, I'm trying to sleep here," said Steve in his annoyingly squeaky voice. "What's all the noise about?"

Down the hall they heard a door open, followed by a mysterious sound.

"It's her. It's the woman," said Maggie, hiding behind her father. "She's coming to get me."

"I think that's Coral on her scooter," said Mr. Cheeseman. "We'd better hide Pinky." Quickly, Jough grabbed Pinky, lifting her onto the bed and pulling the covers up over her head.

"Is everything okay in there, Mr. Stapler?" Coral asked through the door.

Mr. Cheeseman opened the door to reveal Coral sitting on her scooter. Her face was shiny and scrubbed and her hair was full of curlers the size of cucumbers.

"Sorry to wake you, Coral," said Mr. Cheeseman. "But my daughter says she saw a woman standing in her room."

"Not standing," said Maggie. "Roller-skating."

"Oh," said Coral with a chuckle. "Looks like you've had a visit from our resident ghost."

"You have a ghost?" said Mr. Cheeseman.

"I'm afraid so," said Coral. "That's why there are always so many rooms available. Word gets out, you know."

"I'm sorry," said Maggie. "But this didn't look like any ghost I've ever seen on TV or in the movies. Those ghosts are always dressed in flowing white gowns. This woman was wearing a lime green tube top and short, cut-off jeans. She was skating back and forth on pink roller skates."

"That's her all right," said Coral. "I've only owned this

bed-and-breakfast for five years but apparently she's been haunting the place since the mid-1970s. She's harmless, really. Legend has it she was a woman who liked to roller-skate around the house and, one day, got too close to the cellar stairs."

"That's horrible," said Mr. Cheeseman.

"Isn't it? Anyway, I've been meaning for some time now to have something done about it, but there are always so many other little fix-ups to do. Leaky faucets, loose floor boards, burned-out lightbulbs. Leaves a person very little time for things like exorcisms."

"I see," said Mr. Cheeseman.

Just then, Pinky let out a muffled bark from beneath the covers.

"What was that?" asked Coral. "That noise. It sounded like a dog barking."

Jough gave Mr. Cheeseman a worried look.

"Yes," said Mr. Cheeseman. "It sounded exactly like a dog barking. And quite frankly, I am outraged."

"What?" said Coral, taken aback.

"That's right," said Mr. Cheeseman. "This has gone too far. Charging people good money to stay in a house that is haunted by a ghost is one thing. But charging people good money to stay in a house haunted by two ghosts is quite another."

"Two ghosts?"

"Yes. The ghost of a woman in a tube top and the ghost of a barking dog. Why, I have a good mind to complain to the authorities."

"Now, now, there won't be any need for that, Mr. Stapler," said Coral. "Let's just all calm down. Try and get some rest and we can discuss it in the morning."

"I think that's a good idea," said Mr. Cheeseman. "Good night, Coral."

"Good night," said Coral, suspiciously eyeing a somewhat dog-shaped lump beneath the covers as she turned her scooter around and ran into the wall. "Oh, pumpkins!"

When Mr. Cheeseman was certain that Coral had returned to her own room, he shut the door.

"Are you okay, Maggie?"

"I'm scared," she said, hugging her father tightly. "I've never seen a ghost before."

"Neither have I," said Mr. Cheeseman. "I imagine it must have been quite terrifying. But according to Coral, this particular ghost is pretty harmless."

"Harmless or not, I am not going back into that room," said Maggie.

"I understand. Gerard?" Mr. Cheeseman said with a grin. "Still want your own room?"

"I don't know," said Gerard. "What's a tube top?"

"I'll take the room," said Jough.

SOME SPIRITUAL ADVICE ON DEALING WITH GHOSTS

For the record, I do not frighten easily. The following is a complete, unabridged list of things that scare me.

1) Tornadoes
2) Sharks
3) Tornadoes full of sharks
4) Intermittent windshield wipers
5) Ghosts

Though all frightening in their own special way, only one of the above is capable of giving me the creeps, the willies, and the heebie-jeebies all at the same time, and that is a ghost.

I saw my first ghost when I was just ten years old. I awoke one night to find an unearthly presence at the foot of my bed. Startled, I jumped out of bed and immediately fell to my knees and prayed that I had not fractured my kneecaps. Anyone who has ever fallen to his knees knows exactly what I'm talking about.

And as I knelt there, in the middle of my room, praying for pain relief and for that ghost to go away, he turned to me and spoke five simple words. He said, "Never take advice from anyone."

And just like that, he disappeared and never showed himself to me again. But I took his words to be a sign that I should never take advice from others but should, instead, pursue a career in the dispensation of advice. And so, my advice to you regarding ghosts is to always listen to them carefully. They may be telling you something very important.

CHAPTER 18

Mr. 5 sat at a booth in a roadside diner with Mr. 88, Mr. 29, and Mr. 207. Despite the fact that his breakfast was perfectly delicious, Mr. 5 was not happy. For nearly two years now he had been tracking his prey, but on this morning, he had absolutely no clue as to where Mr. Cheeseman might be. He knew it wouldn't be long before Mr. 1 would demote him to the lowly double- or triple-figure status of his dining companions, who were in the midst of a very meaningful discussion.

"Now what about pulverizing? What is that?" asked Mr. 207.

"Pulverizing is what I'm going to do to all of you if you don't shut up this instant," said Mr. 5, slamming his juice glass down onto the table for emphasis. "We had them. We were so close this time and once again they've completely vanished."

"Maybe they used the LVR," said Mr. 207 through a mouthful of buttered toast. "It's possible. I mean, if the whole reason we've been after them all these years is because they have a machine that can enable time travel, then it's quite logical to assume they may have already used it for that purpose."

"You'd better hope that's not the case," said Mr. 5. "Because if the LVR is already working, they're liable to go back to a certain time in history that none of us would like to revisit. Remember, you're all accomplices in the death of Mrs. Cheeseman. It was you, Mr. 88, who spiked her coffee that morning. And it was you, Mr. 29, who picked the lock on the door to let him in."

"What about me?" asked Mr. 207. "I was sick that week. Sore throat."

"You'll have more than a sore throat if you don't stop talking," said Mr. 5. "If we don't find them before they perfect the LVR, we could all find ourselves in a great deal of trouble."

"I told you we should have taken care of the whole family," said Mr. 88.

"And that's exactly why you are where you are today," hissed Mr. 5. "Because of idiotic statements like that. Don't you realize that we need Mr. Cheeseman alive? Even if we had the LVR, he's the only person who knows the computer code to make it work."

When Mr. 5 and the others had finished their breakfast, they walked out to the car just as a school bus was pulling into the parking lot. They watched as several odd-looking people got off the bus.

"Look at that," said Mr. 5 to his friends.

"No kidding," said Mr. 207. "That beard is out of control."

"No, you moron. I'm talking about the earmuffs. I've only ever seen earmuffs like that on one other person."

"The Cheeseman kid," said Mr. 88.

"Exactly."

As Jibby and the rest of his crew walked toward the diner, they found their path suddenly blocked by four men they had never seen before.

"Excuse me," said Mr. 5. "Sorry to bother you. I couldn't help but notice those exquisite earmuffs you're wearing. Do you mind telling me where you got them?"

"Sure," said Dizzy. "I got them from my friend Ethan."

Mr. 5's eyebrow raised involuntarily. "Ethan, you say. Any idea where we might find this Ethan fellow?"

"Well, the last time I saw them—"

"That's enough, Dizzy," Jibby interrupted, then turned to address Mr. 5 and his friends. "Who are you, anyway?"

"Just a guy with cold ears, that's all," said Mr. 5.

"It's the middle of June," said Three-Eyed Jake.

"Tell that to your buddy," said Mr. 5, nodding toward Dizzy.

"Oh, these earmuffs aren't for keeping your ears warm," said Dizzy. "They were invented by Ethan so that people like me—"

"Okay, that's it, Dizzy," said Jibby. "I am officially revoking your speaking privileges."

"But—"

"Effective immediately."

"I don't see what the big deal is," said Mr. 5. "I was just

admiring the earmuffs and wanted to know where I might get a pair for myself."

"We don't know," said Jibby.

"So you have no idea where Ethan Cheeseman is right now?"

"That's funny," said Jibby. "We never told you our friend's last name."

"I'm sure you must have," said Mr. 5.

"I don't think so. Now stand aside. We're going to get some breakfast."

"I'm afraid I can't let you go until I get a little more information," said Mr. 5, who nodded to Mr. 88, who responded to the nod by pulling a handgun from a shoulder holster beneath his jacket.

"Now wait just a minute here," said Jibby.

"No, you wait just a minute," said Mr. 5. "If you don't tell us what we need to know, the only breakfast you and your little band of freaks will be eating is through a straw. Is that understood?"

Jibby looked at the gun and then back at Mr. 5.

"If you're gonna shoot us, you best do it now and get it over with. But just to advise you, you may get some of us, but you won't get us all. And if you don't get us all, that's one living enemy you'll wish you never made. And one more thing. If you ever threaten me again, it'll be the last time. Now if you'll excuse us."

Jibby pushed his way past Mr. 5 and marched up to the diner while the others followed. Mr. 88 stared at Mr. 5

with a look that seemed to say "Well? Should I shoot them?"

Mr. 5 responded by storming off across the parking lot. Mr. 88 shrugged and retired the gun to his holster, then joined the others in following Mr. 5 to the car.

Inside the diner, Jibby and his friends watched Mr. 5 and the others.

"What do you think?" asked Jake.

"I think Mr. Cheeseman and his children might be in even more trouble than we are," said Jibby. "Those guys are bad news."

Jough, Maggie, and Gerard were sitting on the creaky porch swing when Mr. Cheeseman drove into the driveway and got out of the car with Pinky right behind him.

"Good news," he said. "I think I found the perfect place for us."

"You mean we get to stay in this town?" asked Jough.

"Why not? It's nice and quiet and Pinky hasn't growled since yesterday."

For a brief moment the children forgot all about ghosts on roller skates and government agents and international superspies and let out a cheer, happy that, for the next little while at least, they would not be living in their car.

Mr. Cheeseman warned the children that the house he had picked out was rather small because, after being on the run for so long, money was tight and it was all they could afford.

As they drove to the house, they passed a large empty field that until very recently had been home to an apple orchard. One day, large yellow machines came and removed all of the trees so houses could be built in their place. The machines then leveled out the ground and began digging a series of rectangular holes, each about four feet deep and roughly the width and length of an average-sized house. Of course the dirt had to go somewhere and next to each hole was a huge mound of cool, damp earth.

"Did you see that?" said Gerard as they passed the field. "There must be a zillion dirt clods there."

"A gazillion," said Steve.

"A Brazilian," said Gerard, who was especially delighted to find that the field was only a half block from the small pink house Mr. Cheeseman had chosen as their new home.

Mr. Cheeseman had hardly come to a stop in the driveway when the children bolted from the car and ran through the empty house, which smelled like wet paint and carpet cleaner. Jough and Gerard raced to the bedroom facing the front yard and declared it theirs. Maggie ran to the bedroom facing the back and claimed it for herself. Pinky ran to the bathroom and drank from the toilet.

"Well, what do you think?" Mr. Cheeseman asked his children.

"You're right, it is a little small," said Maggie. "But it's . . . cozy, I suppose."

The house was very clean and very well maintained. The backyard smelled strongly of the bright pink lilacs that grew up against the fence.

159

"I chose it for the double garage and for the neighborhood. The schools are supposed to be very good."

"What about the dirt clods?" said Gerard.

"Uh . . . yes," said Mr. Cheeseman. "That was a very important consideration. Plus, there's a nice park right down the street."

"Is there a baseball diamond?" asked Jough. "At the park?"

"There are three," said Mr. Cheeseman with a smile. "Now, we should be able to get some furniture delivered in the next few days, but in the meantime, I'm afraid we'll be sleeping on the floor."

This was another reason money was tight. Each time Mr. Cheeseman packed up his family and moved them to a new location he had to buy new furniture, which he usually found at any number of local secondhand stores.

"Can we get bunk beds this time?" Gerard pleaded hopefully.

"No," said Jough. "You toss and turn when you sleep and shake the bed all night. Besides, I don't want your bubble gum dropping onto my head."

For the next few nights, they all slept on the floor in their sleeping bags. Gerard talked Mr. Cheeseman into setting up one of the tents in the boys' room so he could at least pretend he was camping out. When the furniture finally arrived, they unpacked their things and did their best to make the place their home.

Maggie unpacked her books, her hair-care products, and her archery equipment. Jough unpacked his clothes and his baseball glove. Gerard unpacked his toys and his presidential dirt clod collection.

"Darn it," he said as he lined each dirt clod up on his new dresser. "Every time we have to move, one of them ends up damaged. Look, Grover Cleveland's beard broke off."

Jough took the dirt clod from Gerard and examined it briefly.

"That is a shame," said Jough, trying to sound sincere. "But now it looks just like Ty Cobb."

"Who's Ty Cobb?"

"He was a famous baseball player."

"But I don't like sports."

"That's ridiculous," said Jough. "How can you like dirt and not like sports?"

"I don't like dirt," said Gerard. "I only like dirt *clods*. There's a difference."

When they had finally gotten the house in order, Mr. Cheeseman began the arduous task of reassembling the LVR so that, once he was able to figure out the formula, it would be ready to go.

In the meantime, the children were becoming accustomed to their new home and their new town. Being that they were smart, pleasant, witty, attractive, polite, and relatively odor free, they all made friends quite easily.

The first to make a friend was Jough. One Sunday afternoon he wanted nothing more than to play catch. He got out his baseball glove and ball but found that Mr. Cheeseman was hard at work in the garage, Gerard was hunting for dirt clods at the construction site down the street, and Maggie was, well, the chances of Maggie agreeing to play catch were about the same as Jough agreeing to put on a tutu and dance *Swan Lake.* Though she was by no means a girlie-girl, baseball was of absolutely no interest to her.

Not to be denied, Jough took his glove and his ball to the front yard, where he proceeded to throw the ball high into the air, letting it bounce off the sloped roof and into his awaiting glove. After ten or so minutes of this, Jough looked over to see a boy just about his own age standing at the edge of the yard.

He was the most well-dressed boy Jough had ever seen. His hair was short and tidy. He wore dark blue shorts with a matching blue shirt, white socks, and shiny brown leather shoes.

"Hello there," the boy said with a nod.

"Hello," said Jough.

"Do you like baseball?"

"Yeah," said Jough. "I'd like to pitch in the World Series someday."

"You must be pretty good then."

"To tell you the truth, I'm not sure whether I am or not," said Jough. "My family moves around so much that I hardly ever get to play. But I can throw a screwball. My dad's a physicist and he taught me how to throw all kinds of pitches using scientific principles. How about you? Do you play?"

"I play pinochle, backgammon, three-dimensional chess,

and the bass drum in the school band," said the boy. "But no baseball. Not anymore. My dad made me sign up for baseball last year, but I was absolutely terrible."

"Oh come on," said Jough. "I'm sure you weren't that bad."

"You don't understand," said the boy. "My dad would come to the games and tell the other dads that I had a wooden leg."

"Oh."

"And a glass eye."

"I see."

"And that I was adopted. Then, on the way home after the game, he would make fun of me and remind me of everything I did wrong, which was, well, everything."

"Wow, that's too bad," said Jough. "I guess I'm lucky that my dad has always been very supportive."

"Aw, it's just as well," said the boy. "I'm allergic to grass. And plants. And most kinds of dirt."

"So, in other words, you're allergic to . . . Earth?"

"Pretty much. Except for the parts that have been paved over. Thank goodness for the indoors."

"That must be awful."

"I take medicine. I'm Elliot, by the way," said the boy as he walked across the yard with his well-dressed arm fully extended. "Elliot Walsingham."

Jough took Elliot's hand and shook. "I'm Jough. Nice to meet you."

"It was only a matter of time," said Elliot. "I live in that big green house just down the street. The one with the blue convertible in the driveway. I'm sure you've heard me practicing the bass drum."

"No, actually I haven't," said Jough. "I guess we've been busy getting moved in and everything."

"Oh, well, I'm sure you will hear me eventually. It's my dream to one day play bass drum for the London Philharmonic. So where are you from?"

"That's hard to say," said Jough. "We've moved around so much, I sort of forget where we're from."

"Is your dad in the army or something?"

"No. It's a long story. Maybe I'll tell it to you one day."

"Maybe Saturday," said Elliot.

"Saturday? Why Saturday?"

"That's when they're holding baseball tryouts. I thought maybe I could go with you. Show you around a bit."

"Sure," said Jough. "That'd be great."

"Maybe when you make it to the big leagues, I could be your agent," said Elliot. "I'm very good with numbers."

"Sure," said Jough. "If I ever need an agent, I'll definitely keep you in mind."

While Jough was becoming acquainted with Elliot, Gerard was busy in the field at the end of the street, picking through the giant mounds of dirt. It was Sunday, so no construction work was being done, which gave Gerard complete freedom to look for interestingly shaped dirt clods at his own pace. Just as he picked one up that looked remarkably like former U.S. president Millard Fillmore, another dirt clod, shaped like no one in particular, came sailing through the air and hit him in the side of the head, splattering into hundreds of much smaller dirt clods as it did.

"Ouch," Gerard cried as he dropped the Millard Fillmore dirt clod and rubbed his head. He wheeled around to see two boys, each about the same age as himself, standing about twenty feet away. Though it was hard to get a good look at them with the sun at their backs, Gerard could see that in each boy's hand was a dirt clod.

"Hey, you hit me," Gerard said.

"That's right," said the taller of the two boys. "And we'll do it again if you don't stay away from our fort."

"I'm not after your fort," said Gerard. "I'm just looking for dirt clods. I don't even know where your stupid fort is."

The two boys looked at each other, trying to decide whether Gerard was telling the truth. They decided he must have been, because if he *had* actually seen their glorious fort, he wouldn't dare to call it stupid. The boys walked toward Gerard but kept their dirt clods in hand, just in case.

"You're that new kid, aren't you," said the shorter of the two boys. "What's that on your hand?"

"This is Steve," said Gerard.

"Hello there," said Steve, in his squeaky sock-puppet voice.

"I saw your lips move," the taller of the two boys said, pointing at Gerard's mouth.

"So?" said Gerard. "I never said I was a ventrickolist. I'm just a normal kid. And Steve's just an old sock puppet."

"Hey! I heard that," said Steve.

The boys laughed.

"He may be just an old sock puppet," said the shorter of the two. "But you're not a normal kid, that's for sure."

"See?" said Steve. "I told you you weren't normal."

The boys laughed again, then introduced themselves as Tommy and Danny Codgill, Tommy being the taller of the two, Danny being his slightly shorter, slightly younger brother.

"You wanna see our fort?" Tommy said.

"It's a secret spy fort," added Danny.

"Sure," said Gerard. "I'd love to see it."

"Me too," said Steve.

"Okay. But until we're sure we can trust you, you've gotta put on this blindfold until we get there," said Tommy, producing a red bandanna from the pocket of his shorts.

"Wait a minute," said Gerard. "How do I know I can trust you? Once I'm blindfolded, you could lead me right into one of these big holes and I could break my leg."

"We wouldn't do that," said Danny. "We won't do anything that might hurt you. We promise."

"Just five minutes ago you hit me in the head with a dirt clod," Gerard reminded them.

"He's right about that," Tommy said to his younger brother. "All right then. Let's forget the blindfold. But you gotta swear not to tell anyone where the secret spy fort is located."

"I swear," said Gerard.

"Me too," said Steve.

As it turns out, the fort was located not far from where

they were standing, which might explain why Tommy and Danny were suspicious of Gerard's reasons for being in the area. It was hidden amid a patch of tall weeds. The fort was constructed mostly of plywood, rusty nails, and tarpaper.

"This is it," said Tommy. "The secret fort."

"Cool," said Gerard. "Where'd you get the stuff to make it?"

Tommy and Danny looked at each other moving only their eyes. "Borrowed it," they said in unison.

"From the construction site," said Tommy. "They'll never miss it."

The secret spy fort was only about three feet tall, so even someone as short as Gerard had to crawl on his hands and knees to get inside. And, once inside, Gerard was able to see, with the help of the official fort flashlight, all of the fabulous secret spy equipment therein.

There were the secret spy fort binoculars, which were constructed of two empty toilet paper tubes glued together. There was the secret spy fort walkie-talkie. Just one. The other had gone missing months ago and this one had no batteries, so it was strictly ornamental at this point. And there was the official spy fort slingshot, suitable for firing rocks, marbles, or dirt clods at any and all intruders.

Tommy and Danny each took a seat on upside-down plastic pickle barrels that served as the official fort chairs, of which there were only two, which left Gerard to sit in the dirt.

"Well, you were right," he said, taking in his surroundings. "It is a pretty cool fort. But you could use some better spy equipment. I mean, look at these binoculars. They're just two toilet paper tubes glued together."

"So," said Tommy, snatching the paper binoculars from Gerard's unappreciative hands. "What do you know about spy equipment anyway?"

"I know a lot about it," Gerard shot back. "My family is on the run from government agents."

"You're lying."

Now, Gerard knew better than to divulge family secrets but he was not about to stand by and be called a liar by a couple of boys with binoculars made of toilet paper tubes.

"I'm not lying."

"Why would government agents be chasing after you and your dumb family anyway?" Danny sneered.

"Because my father is a scientist and has invented something they can't wait to get their hands on. And there are other people, too, not just the government. The people who killed our mom. They'll do anything they can to steal the invention. We've been traveling across the country, trying to stay ahead of them so that my dad can finish building it."

"It's true," said Steve.

"Okay," said Tommy. "And what does this machine do that's so great?"

"I can't tell you," said Gerard. "It's top secret."

The two boys did not look impressed. In fact, they looked downright annoyed.

"You have to leave now," said Danny. "We don't allow liars in our fort."

"Shut up," shouted Gerard. "I'm not a liar!" Gerard punctuated his assertion by reaching out and shoving Danny off his pickle drum and into the dirt.

"Okay, that's it," said Danny. "Let's fight."

Besides the fact that Gerard was outnumbered two to one, he really had no desire to fight Tommy and Danny. In fact, all he really wanted was to make new friends and to become a member of their stupid spy fort even if it was equipped with binoculars made from toilet paper tubes. He decided to take another approach toward a friendly resolution of the situation.

"Okay," said Gerard. "We can fight if you want. But before we do, I just have one question."

"What's that?" asked Danny with a smirkish look.

"Does your spy fort have any arrowheads?"

"Arrowheads?" asked Tommy, suddenly less interested in the potential for a fight. "You mean like real ones?"

"I mean like this," said Gerard, reaching into his pocket and pulling out the arrowhead.

The boys gasped as they moved closer to Gerard and marveled at the small stone artifact as if it were the world's rarest of diamonds.

"Where did you get that?" said Danny.

"I got it from a cowboy named Buck."

"I'm serious. Where did you get it?"

"I told you. From a cowboy named Buck. He's a poet, too. We met him when we were camping out in the desert. We helped him with his poetry so he gave me, my brother, and my sister each an arrowhead."

"We need to make a bow right away," said Tommy excitedly. "Then we can try it out and see if it works."

"It'll help protect us from intruders," said Danny.

"And we can use it for hunting," said Tommy.

"No, no, it's not for shooting or hunting," said Gerard. "It's too valuable for that. It's for saving. And for good luck."

Tommy looked at Danny and shrugged. Danny shrugged back.

"Okay," said Tommy. "You can be a member of our secret spy fort. But you have to swear to follow the special fort rules."

Tommy went on to explain the many rules involved in becoming a member of the secret spy fort. These included promising to never divulge the fort's location to anyone (especially teachers, parents, and girls), pledging to protect the fort from any and all intruders, fighting to the death if necessary, and demonstrating that you know at least three swear words.

"I do so know three swear words," said Gerard.

"Okay," said Tommy, "let's hear 'em."

"Well, I'm not going to say them out loud. I don't think my dad would like that very much. And my mom is watching me from up in heaven, so I don't want to disappoint her. How about if I just say that I know them?"

Once more Tommy looked at Danny, who shrugged again. Gerard casually tossed the arrowhead into the air and caught it.

"Okay," said Tommy. "You're in. But you have to bring the arrowhead with you whenever you come to the fort."

"Don't worry. I keep it with me wherever I go. I told you, it's good luck."

In a brief ceremony involving dirt, spit, and one of the plastic pickle barrels used for ritualistic drumming, Gerard was officially sworn in as the newest member of the secret spy fort. The three boys talked for hours after that. Gerard learned that his two new friends, together with their mother and father and older sister, lived on the other side of the field that had once been an apple orchard.

They said their father was a policeman, which made Gerard even a little sorrier that he had told them about the LVR and about the government agents and all that. He was glad now that they hadn't believed his story and he promised himself that from that day forward he would keep his big, fat mouth shut.

CHAPTER 19

While Jough was busy making friends with Elliot and Gerard was busy revealing family secrets to two kids who had hit him in the head with a dirt clod, Maggie was taking Pinky for a walk and exploring her new neighborhood.

Because Pinky was in a permanent state of extreme hairlessness, this activity required serious preparation, especially in the month of June, when the sun's rays were very direct. Before Pinky could go out, Maggie first had to coat the animal with a generous layer of sunscreen lotion, a process that Pinky enjoyed slightly less than having the vet check her for ringworm.

Still, she preferred it to the only alternatives, which were to either stay in the house all day or to go out wearing a bizarre-looking contraption Mr. Cheeseman had invented called the Bum-brella, which consisted of a harness that attached to the dog's backside into which a large parasol could be inserted, keeping Pinky constantly in the shade.

Luckily for Pinky, Maggie patently refused to be seen in public walking a dog with an umbrella protruding from its bum. Even without the Bum-brella, Maggie got some rather strange looks just by walking a dog with no hair. One of the looks she got was from a young girl sitting on the sidewalk in front of a two-story gray and white house.

With different colors of chalk, the girl was creating a very impressive piece of artwork right there on that sidewalk. Maggie and Pinky stopped for a moment to watch as the girl put the finishing touches on a drawing of nothing in particular that was still quite fabulous to look at.

"That's very nice," said Maggie. "I like the colors."

"Your dog has no hair," the girl said with a slight giggle.

"I know. She lost all her hair years ago. It's a long story," said Maggie, trying not to think about the terrible circumstances that lead to Pinky's irreversible baldness.

"She looks like a pig," said the girl.

"She eats like a pig, too. And she drinks from the toilet."

"That's funny. I once had a cat who liked to chase cars."

"Really? What happened to him?"

"He liked to chase cars."

"Oh. I see."

The girl gave Pinky an affectionate pat until she realized her hands were covered with colored chalk and now so was Pinky's head.

"Sorry about that," she said, standing up and wiping her hands on her white denim shorts, which were white no longer.

The first thing Maggie noticed about the girl was that, unless she was actually a thirty-year-old woman posing as a young girl, she was very tall for her age.

"My name's Aurora. Aurora Codgill."

"I'm Maggie. I just moved here a couple days ago. We live in a pink house on the other side of the field."

"Yes, I know that house very well. The Blithedales used to live there. They had to move because they had way too many children for such a small house. Five children. And do you know that they all had names beginning with the letter *L*? Larry, Lisa, Leroy, Lonnie, and Lucille. Their parents were Leonard and Linda and they had a little black dog named Licorice. Is that the most ridiculous thing you've ever heard or what?"

"I suppose it is," agreed Maggie, who had actually heard things far more ridiculous than that. "And I can see how the house would be too small for them. I live there with my dad and my two brothers."

"I'm just glad there are more kids in the neighborhood. Before the Blithedales lived there it was the Parkhills, who had just one child, and before that it was Mr. and Mrs. Nuñez, who had no children at all."

"You seem to know a lot about our house," said Maggie.

"I know a lot about all the houses in this neighborhood. I've lived here all my life, so I've been inside most of them, including your house. Lucille and I used to play together in the backyard."

"Well, maybe you'd like to come over sometime."

"Sure," said Aurora. "If you don't mind being seen with someone so freakishly tall."

"What? Oh don't be silly. You're not freakishly tall. I mean, you are very tall, but I wouldn't say freakishly so."

"It's okay," said Aurora. "I know I am. That's why my two creepy little brothers call me Aurorasaurus. They think I look like a dinosaur."

"I don't think you look like a dinosaur at all. I think you look pretty. Besides, I bet you can run awfully fast with those long legs."

"Not fast enough to catch my little brothers, unfortunately."

"Little brothers can be so annoying sometimes, can't they?"

"You can say that again. Luckily my brothers spend most of their time in their stupid old fort out in the field. In fact, they're there right now, so it's safe if you'd like to come in for a glass of lemonade."

"I'd love to," said Maggie. "But Pinky . . ."

"She can come too."

Inside, the house was clean and tidy and smelled like food, though which kind of food Maggie couldn't be sure.

"Would you like to see my room?" asked Aurora.

Aurora's room was covered, wall-to-wall and ceiling-to-floor, with the many colorful paintings and drawings she had done, some landscapes, some still life, and others, like the one on the sidewalk, of nothing in particular.

"Wow," said Maggie. "Did you do all these?"

"Do you like them?"

"Like them? They're fantastic."

"Thanks," said Aurora shyly. "I'd like to be an artist when I grow up."

"When you grow up?" said Maggie. "You're an artist now."

"Thanks," said Aurora. "But I mean for real. I would live in a little house by the sea and I would sell my paintings to people from New York and London and Portugal."

"I wish I could do anything as well as you paint."

"I'm sure there must be plenty of things you can do well," said Aurora.

"I guess I'm pretty good at algebra, geography, physics, and archery."

"Archery? You mean like bows and arrows? I would love to learn how to do that."

"Hey, how about this? You teach me how to paint, and I'll teach you how to shoot."

"Deal," said Aurora, reaching out with her right hand.

As Maggie shook hands with her new friend, she noticed another painting, sitting on the floor. It was a portrait of a handsome young man.

"Who's that?" she asked.

"Oh, that," said Aurora, looking somewhat embarrassed. "That's Dean Greenfield."

"Who's Dean Greenfield?"

"Just a boy in my class. I used to like him, I guess."

"Oh. What happened?"

"Well, let's just say he was not quite as taken with me as I was with him. In fact, he was the first to call me Aurorasaurus. Now he's got everyone saying it, including my stupid little brothers."

"He sounds absolutely horrible," said Maggie. "What are you going to do with the painting?"

"I don't know. I thought I might paint a pair of goat horns on him. Or maybe give him buckteeth and a unibrow."

"I have a better idea," said Maggie. Before she could expound upon this, she looked down and noticed that Pinky was no longer by her side. She called for the dog but Pinky didn't come. Then she heard a very familiar sound and followed it down the hallway, where she found Pinky, in the guest bathroom, very happily drinking from the toilet.

"Pinky, get out of there," she scolded. "Sorry about that, Aurora."

"No problem," said Aurora, who found the whole thing quite funny and was just happy to have met someone who loved her artwork and did not think she, in any way, resembled a dinosaur.

As Pinky trotted out of the bathroom well hydrated, Maggie noticed a photograph of Aurora's parents hanging in the hallway, her father dressed in a policeman's uniform, his large dimpled chin looking very much like a baby's bare bottom.

"So your dad's a police officer, I see."

"He's a police captain, actually."

"That seems like an exciting job."

"Not in this town it's not," said Aurora. "There's no crime here. Of course my dad says that will all change once they finish building that big factory outside of town."

"What kind of factory?"

"I'm not sure," said Aurora. "I think they're going to make microwave ovens."

CHAPTER 20

That night at dinner, everyone seemed in good spirits. Maggie, Jough, and Gerard had all made new friends and Mr. Cheeseman was nearly finished reassembling the LVR into its oblong, disco-ball shape.

"I'm sorry I've been so busy these past few days," he said between bites of frozen pizza. Actually, that's not entirely accurate. The pizza was not frozen. In fact, it was quite hot and melty but had at one time been frozen when Mr. Cheeseman first purchased it at the supermarket. "And I'm sorry that I haven't had much of a chance to find out how you're all settling in."

"I'm settling in great," said Gerard. "I met two boys about my age and they let me join their secret spy fort."

"Secret spy fort?" said Maggie. "Are their names Tommy and Danny by any chance?"

"Yeah. How did you know?" Gerard asked suspiciously. "Have you been spying on us?"

"No, I have not been spying on you. In fact, I can't think

of anything I would like to do less. It's just that I made friends with their sister, Aurora, today. She's very nice. And a very good artist."

"You must be talking about Aurorasaurus," said Gerard.

"That's not nice at all," Maggie said. "I can tell you right now that nickname is very hurtful to Aurora and if you call her that again, I will punch you."

Gerard suddenly looked a little embarrassed. "I didn't make up the name. I was just repeating what I heard."

"Parrots repeat what they hear," said Mr. Cheeseman. "And they have a brain the size of a walnut. I suggest you choose your words more carefully. And Magenta-Jean Jurgenson, there will be no punching your brother or anyone else. Is that understood?"

"Okay. No punching."

"Good. Now what about you, Jough? How are you getting along here?"

"Well, I met the boy from the big green house down the street today. His name is Elliot. He's kind of weird but very nice. He said that baseball tryouts are this Saturday."

"Are you going to give it a shot?" asked Mr. Cheeseman.

"I don't know," said Jough. "I would hate to let my teammates down if suddenly we had to pack up and move again in the middle of the season."

"I think you should go for it," said Mr. Cheeseman. "I've got a good feeling about this town and I've never been closer to making the LVR fully operational. The problem is still the code. I don't suppose any of you have had a chance to try and crack it."

Mr. Cheeseman reached into his pocket and pulled out the mint green piece of paper upon which was written the incomplete code.

"Sorry, I haven't," said Maggie.

"Not yet," said Jough.

"I have," said Steve confidently. "And I think I've got it. When danger lurks and your heart is racing . . . dial 911 and get the police to take care of the danger and an ambulance to take care of your racing heart."

No one said anything at first, except Pinky, who, as usual, snarled at the mangy sock puppet for whom her dislike grew daily.

"That's . . . not bad," said Mr. Cheeseman. "I'll give it a shot and see what happens. Anyone else?"

"I don't know," said Jough. "It's a tough one. I mean it could be anything, right?"

"And what happens if we never figure it out?" asked Maggie.

"Then I'm afraid I'll have to try and hack into the mainframe and create an entirely new code. Or, worse yet, build an entirely new computer. And that could take a year or more. Your mother was much better with computers than I am. But don't worry. I have faith that we'll crack the code soon."

Mr. Cheeseman spoke with confidence but secretly wondered if he would ever get the LVR working and, if so, would he be able to keep it out of the hands of those with evil intent, those who, as each day passed, were getting closer and closer.

Saturday arrived and by midmorning the sun had risen in the sky like a 4.5-billion-year-old, average-sized star burning at roughly 10,000 degrees Kelvin at its core.

It was a perfect day for a baseball tryout and Jough was happy to find Elliot waiting for him when he left the house with his baseball glove tucked under his arm and his black curly hair bunching out from beneath his cap.

"Did you get a good night's sleep?" asked Elliot. "It's important that you be well rested."

"Don't worry," said Jough. "I feel fine."

"Okay, but you might want to consider smiling more. Likability is an important factor in securing lucrative endorsement deals."

This did make Jough smile. "I haven't even played my first game of organized baseball and already you're thinking about endorsement deals?"

"It's never too early to start working on your public image. Have you considered adopting a child from a foreign country? And you may want to lose the mustache. Makes you look just a little bit sinister. Just saying."

"You're really taking this agent thing seriously," said Jough, rubbing his barely-there mustache.

"I take everything seriously," said Elliot. "Look at this."

Elliot reached into his pocket and produced a business card and handed it to Jough. The card read:

> ## Walsingham Group
> ## Sports Management
>
> *Elliot Walsingham*
> *President*

"Nice," said Jough, wondering whether he should be flattered or disturbed. "Very nice."

"Thank you," said President Walsingham. "I've drawn up a contract for you to look at later. You're a minor, so it'll have to be signed by your parents. Will they be coming out to the tryouts today?"

"No, my dad's got too much work to do. But he promised he'll be at all my games to cheer me on."

"Oh. How about your mom?"

"No. She, uh . . . she died. Two years ago."

"Wow, that's funny," said Elliot.

"Funny? What's so funny about it?" snapped Jough.

"No, no, I didn't mean funny. I meant it's strange because my mother died, too. When I was just six. She was in a car accident."

"I'm sorry to hear that," said Jough, suddenly sorry he had spoken so roughly to his new friend and possible future agent.

"It's okay," said Elliot. "You get used to it as time goes by."

But Jough didn't think he'd ever get used to it.

The baseball field was teeming with kids Jough's age, all warming up and milling about. Many of them were there with their fathers, which made Jough feel a bit envious, though he did appear to be the only kid there with his own personal manager in tow.

"I'm glad you're trying out and not me," said Elliot. "Last year I got so nervous I threw up on home plate. Just the thought of all those people watching me was too much."

There would be a lot of people watching. In addition to the prospective players, coaches from every team were there, scouting the talent pool from which they would draft their teams. Among them were: Gino Zaremba, owner and coach of Gino's Pizza; Tyson Pram, owner and coach of Pram's Insurance; and Wendle Endersbee, owner and coach of Wendle's Auto Body Repair.

"Wendle's Auto Body would be a very good fit for us," said Elliot as Jough performed some basic stretches.

"A good fit?" said Jough.

"Yes. Rumor has it that they secretly pay their players. Five dollars if you hit a home run, ten dollars if you hit a car in the parking lot."

Jough tried to ignore Elliot and continued to warm up while waiting patiently until his name was called from the sign-up sheet.

"Jough Psmythe!" bellowed Gino Zaremba, mistakenly pronouncing the *P* in Psmythe.

"Okay," said Elliot. "This is it. Let's show 'em what you

can do. And if you feel like you're going to throw up, just try and convince yourself that you feel fine."

"I do feel fine."

"That's the spirit," said Elliot as he gave Jough a pat on the back and watched nervously while his possible future meal ticket walked to the pitcher's mound.

Coach Zaremba, serving as the home plate umpire, tossed Jough a ball. Jough took the ball and smacked it into his glove a few times just to get the feel of it. He dug in and looked to home plate, where a large brute of a kid was standing with a cocky smile on his big brutish face. In his hands was the biggest bat Jough had ever seen outside of a cartoon. Jough's first thought was, "If this kid hits the ball, it could break a window on the space shuttle."

Jough paused and looked over at Elliot, standing near the dugout.

"Don't worry, Jough," Elliot shouted. "The bigger they are, the harder they fall."

Jough smiled and, with all eyes turned his way, he went into his windup and delivered his first pitch, a screaming fastball. The giant kid at the plate took a giant swing with his giant bat and a loud *thwack!* carried through the air. Everyone looked to the sky to see the ball, but it was nowhere in sight. Could it be the ball was hit so hard and so far that it was invisible to the naked eye? Or could it be that the loud *thwack!* everyone had assumed was the ball hitting the bat was actually the ball hitting the catcher's mitt?

"Strike one!" shouted Coach Zaremba.

The catcher tossed the ball back to Jough while the batter

dug in with his back foot, more determined than ever to impress the coaches and to show Jough he was a better hitter than Jough was a pitcher. Inside his glove, Jough gripped the ball and prepared to send in his secret weapon, the screwball his father taught him to throw using scientific principles. Jough wound up and delivered the pitch, which started out right down the middle, then broke sharply inside.

The batter swung and this time he did hit the ball. Luckily for Jough, he only hit a small portion of the ball, which spun up high into the air, carrying over the chain-link backstop and, with a loud *thunk*, hit a car in the parking lot.

"Yes!" said Coach Wendle Endersbee of Wendle's Auto Body Repair.

"Darn it!" said Coach Tyson Pram, the car's owner.

"Strike two," said Coach Zaremba as he reached into his pocket and pulled out a new ball. He tossed the ball to Jough, who looked to home plate. The batter's face was now beet red with anger and frustration, and Jough knew the boy would be swinging hard. So he dug in, wound up, and threw the ball as slowly as he could toward the catcher's anxious mitt.

The batter swung his cartoonish bat with all his might, twirling like a cyclone as he missed the ball by a good three feet and raised a cloud of dust that could choke a Tibetan yak. He threw his giant bat to the ground and stormed off as Jough took a moment to bask in the impromptu applause from his peers.

"Great job," said Elliot as Jough walked back toward the

dugout. "Great pitching, and you didn't even throw up. Nice touch with the smile at the end, too. You came across as very likable."

"Thanks."

"You really caught Coach Wendle's eye. We're in a very good place, I think."

Coach Wendle Endersbee certainly would have chosen Jough after watching him deliver that almost unhittable screwball across the plate with remarkable speed and accuracy. In fact, Jough's pitching impressed all of the coaches there. It just so happened, however, that first pick in this year's draft went to Police Chief Roy Codgill, captain of the local police force and coach of the Police Pals.

"Well, I'd be lying if I didn't say I'm a little disappointed," said Elliot as he and Jough looked at the rosters, which had been posted on the dugout wall. "Due to government cutbacks, the Police Pals are the most underfunded team in the league. It's rumored that some of their equipment is taken from the evidence room."

"Come on," said Jough, shaking his head. "You're making that up."

"It's true. Last year a kid found a clump of hair on the end of his bat."

"Don't believe everything you hear," came a round, hollow voice from behind them.

Jough and Elliot turned to see a very muscular man with thick arms that failed to taper at the wrist, as most arms tend to do. He had a blond crew cut and a large baby's-butt chin.

"Welcome to the Police Pals," said Chief Codgill as he

shook Jough's hand with a grip so strong it made Jough wince.

"Easy on that right hand," said Elliot. "That's going to make us both a lot of money someday."

"Yeah? And who are you?" said Chief Codgill, looking down at Elliot with a bit of a scowl.

"Name's Elliot Walsingham, president of Walsingham Group Sports Management. My card."

Elliot presented Chief Codgill with a business card. "Thanks," he said, rather insincerely. "Now if you'll excuse me, I'd like to talk to your client if you don't mind."

"No problem. I'll be right over here if you need me, Jough. And whatever you do, don't sign anything."

"That was some pretty impressive pitching out there today," said Chief Codgill. "I've never met a kid your age who could throw a screwball."

"It's nothing," said Jough modestly. "It's just basic physics, that's all."

"It's just amazing, is what it is. Keep it up and we could win it all this year. Then maybe they'll give us some more money for new equipment."

As Chief Codgill was complimenting Jough on his outstanding pitching ability, his sons, Tommy and Danny, were sitting in their secret spy fort with their newest member, trying to decide what to do with this fabulously sunny day.

"Well, what do you usually do?" asked Gerard as he fiddled with the lone walkie-talkie.

"We usually just hang out here and try to keep intruders away," said Danny.

"Oh. Do you ever get any intruders?"

"Just you," said Tommy. "It's not easy fighting off intruders when no one knows where your fort is."

"Maybe we should tell people where it is," said Gerard. "Then, when they come looking for it, we can fight them off."

"That's not a bad idea," said Tommy. "It would be nice to have someone to throw dirt clods at for a change."

Funny Tommy should say that because, just eighty miles away on a deserted rural highway, there were, heading somewhat in their direction, plenty of people at whom dirt clods should be thrown.

"There will be a parade for us and much money when we return with LVR," said Pavel, his teeth clamped tightly around the butt of a large, smoky cigar as he piloted the little brown car down the highway. He didn't necessarily like cigars but he much preferred the smell of cigars to the combined smell of monkey and fish, two odors that are rarely inhaled in the same breath. "They will treat us like kings, my leetle minkey friend."

Leon expressed his excitement in his usual way, by slapping himself repeatedly on the head. Pavel laughed and bit down hard on the cigar. But his laughter was soon doused by something he saw on the dashboard of his small brown car. What he saw was a red light telling him that his car was overheating. Pavel pounded his fist angrily on the dashboard and cursed in his native language. Leon cursed in his native chimp and Pavel pulled the car over onto the road's gravelly shoulder as steam began to rise up from beneath the hood.

The doors flew open and the angry international super-spy and his trusty sidekick stepped out to get a better look at things. Upon lifting the hood and removing the radiator cap, Pavel realized that the radiator had gone practically bone dry and, to make matters worse, it had done so out in the middle of nowhere.

"This is not happening!" Pavel roared to the heavens. "This is very, very horrible!"

"Wha wha whee!" Leon agreed.

"We are twenty-five miles from next town! Why?" he asked the broken-down car. "Why do you have to break down here? This is very bad and also not so good."

Pavel paced back and forth, cursing under his breath. Leon decided to show support by doing the same.

"We will never be first to get LVR unless we can get car working. But car will not run without water. If only there was lake or river or . . ."

Pavel stopped in midsentence. He had an idea and, by the horrified look on Leon's face, it was obvious that Leon had a pretty good idea what Pavel's idea was.

"Leon, it is only way."

Leon shook his head and tried to keep himself between Pavel and the back door of the little brown car as Pavel walked slowly toward it, eyeing the ten-gallon fish tank resting on the backseat.

"I am sorry, my leetle friend, but you must step aside. One day I will get for you many new feeshes. But now, you must make sacrifice for good of country."

Leon responded by getting down on his hands and knees right there on the side of the road and doing the perfect impression of an angry male hippo.

"I know, I know," said Pavel. "I do not forget you saved Pavel's life. But if Pavel returns home without LVR, Pavel's life will be worth nothing. We will be outcasts, perhaps thrown in prison for the end of times."

Leon sighed and stood up, brushing the dirt from his hands. He looked at Pavel and then into the car at his three little goldfish, swimming happily in complete and utter ignorance. He sighed again, then slowly and reluctantly stepped aside.

"That's my boy. Trust me, you will be big hero. Many statues of you will be built and many songs about you they will sing."

With that, Pavel opened the back door and reached in for the fish tank. A sound, far off in the distance, caused Leon to cock his ear toward the horizon. Could it be? Quickly, he reached over and tugged on Pavel's pant leg.

"Leon, please," said Pavel. "I know you are not happy, but there is no other way."

Leon screamed, hit himself on the head a few times, and pointed frantically down the road in the direction they had come. Pavel looked but he saw nothing. In a moment, though, he too heard something. It was the sound of an approaching car.

"Yes," said Pavel. "Now there is other way. We will be saved and your feeshes will live. And we will be first to get LVR and we will be big heroes. They will write songs about Pavel and Leon."

Leon hugged Pavel tightly around the knees and Pavel patted the happy chimp on the head.

"Come here," said Pavel, extending his hand. Leon took the hand and climbed up Pavel's arm and onto his shoulders. As the car got closer, both Pavel and Leon waved their arms frantically in the air and shouted at the top of their lungs.

"Help! We need help!"

"Whee whaa whoo!"

"Well, would you look at this?" said Aitch Dee as he drove toward Pavel and Leon in his sporty red rental car, red because the rental car company had completely run out of gray cars.

"I don't believe it," said El Kyoo. "Should we arrest them?"

"I would, but they would just slow us down. Besides, I think it'd be a lot more fun to just leave 'em here."

"Sounds good to me," agreed El Kyoo. As the red car blew by, he was overcome with the uncontrollable urge to stick his head out the window and yell, which is exactly what he did. "Hey, Pavel! Get that monkey off your back!"

"I hate those guys," said Pavel as the sporty red car sped away, leaving them stranded in the middle of nowhere.

CHAPTER 21

Pavel fired up the engine and pulled back onto the highway, leaving behind three tiny crosses made of twigs, planted in the gravelly shoulder of the road. Behind those tiny crosses was a miniature plastic replica of the Parthenon, a fitting memorial for those who gave their lives for their country.

"Leon. Please do not be angry with Pavel. It was only way. We must be first to get LVR. You understand, no?"

With a shake of his head, Leon confirmed that he indeed did not understand. He then folded his arms even tighter in the most petulant of ways and looked out the side window as the little brown car limped toward the next town, only fifty-five miles from the Cheesemans' small pink rental house, where Jough was just returning from his highly successful tryout.

"It's a pretty standard contract," said Elliot, handing Jough a sheet of paper. "A straight ten percent commission, so I don't get paid until you get paid."

"I'll look it over," said Jough, who had no intention of looking it over, much less signing it.

"Great," said Elliot. "In the meantime I've got to call the newspaper and make sure they're at your first game."

Inside the little pink house, Mr. Cheeseman had just walked in from the garage to find Gerard in the living room, parked on the secondhand couch, watching the secondhand TV.

"What are you doing watching TV on such a nice day? You should be outdoors, having fun."

"What's so fun about outside?" said Gerard without removing his eyes from the TV.

"Well, isn't your spy fort outside?"

"I already went there. There were no intruders today so we all decided to go home early," said Gerard as he continued to flip through the channels, watching nothing in particular.

"What about hunting for dirt clods? There must be at least a million that you haven't yet looked at."

"That's the problem," said Gerard, rubbing the smooth surface of his lucky arrowhead between his thumb and forefinger. "There are so many that it takes all the fun out of it."

"Well, now that Jough's signed up for baseball, I think we should see about getting you in with the Cub Scouts."

"Really," said Gerard. "Could I?"

"Of course you can."

The door opened and in walked Jough, his glove stuffed beneath his arm. In his right hand was the contract that Elliot had drawn up.

"Well?" said Mr. Cheeseman. "How'd it go?"

"Great. I was the first pick in the entire draft. I'll be playing for the Police Pals."

"The Police Pals, huh?"

"Yeah, our coach is captain of the police force."

"Hey, that's Tommy and Danny's dad," said Gerard. "I'm an official member of their spy fort."

"Small world," said Mr. Cheeseman.

"Well, small town, anyway," said Jough.

"So tell me," said Mr. Cheeseman. "Did you use the screwball?"

"I did," said Jough.

"And?"

"Virtually unhittable."

"That's my boy," said Mr. Cheeseman, slapping his arm around Jough's shoulders. "I wish I could've been there to see it."

"I wish you could've too," said Jough.

"I'm sorry," said Mr. Cheeseman. "I really wanted to get this done. But I promise I'll be at every game. You have my word."

"Thanks, Dad. Our first game is next Saturday."

"Hey, look!" shouted Gerard, suddenly sitting up straight and pointing to the TV. "It's Buck!"

Sure enough, there was Buck Weston standing on stage and reciting one of his poems to a crowd of fellow cowboys

194

and lovers of cowboy poetry as a news reporter talked about the annual contest.

Gerard ran to the window and shouted out to the backyard, where Maggie was practicing her archery, firing arrows into a circular target nailed to the fence.

"Maggie, come here!" Gerard shouted. "It's Buck!"

Her bow in hand, Maggie ran into the house, joining the others just as the reporter, a woman with stiff hair and a microphone in hand began interviewing Buck, who, they noticed, was holding a rather sizable trophy.

"He did it. He really did it," shouted Maggie.

"And how does it feel to be this year's winner of the National Cowboy Poetry Competition?" the reporter asked Buck.

"It feels great," said Buck, the leathery skin of his face stretched tight by an oversized smile. "And I owe it all to my good friends Ethan, Jough, Maggie, and Gerard."

"He remembered us," said Jough.

"Not all of us," said Steve bitterly.

"I hope our paths will cross again one day," said Buck. "But if they do, it won't be out on the trail, 'cause my cowboyin' days are over. From now on, I'm a full-time poet."

A crowd of people standing nearby cheered as Buck raised the trophy above his head.

"Well, what do you know about that," said Mr. Cheeseman. "This day is just full of good news. If it keeps up like this, who knows what else might happen."

It was then that Mr. Cheeseman noticed that Maggie

was holding her bow. "You're not firing that bow in the backyard, are you?"

"Yes, I guess I was," said Maggie.

"Now what have I told you about that, Magenta-Jean Jurgenson? It's too dangerous."

"But I'm a very good shot," Maggie protested.

"I have no doubt that you are. Still, I would like you to practice at the archery range. It's only about a mile from here."

"Okay," said Maggie just as the doorbell rang, saving her from further discussion of the matter.

Mr. Cheeseman walked to the door and opened it to find an old woman with hair as white and as puffy as a single cloud floating through a blue summer sky. She wore glasses in round wire frames and a long blue dress that could best be described as an "old lady dress," complete with white frill around the collar. Her posture was slightly rounded and, in her arms, she held a black and brown Chihuahua. Even though it was quite a warm afternoon, the Chihuahua seemed to be shivering as if it had just eaten a bowl of ice cream while standing in a snowstorm.

"Why, hello there," said the woman. "My name is Mrs. Frampton. I'm head of the neighborhood welcome committee, so welcome to the neighborhood."

Before Mr. Cheeseman could answer, Pinky appeared at his feet and began growling and snarling. Mrs. Frampton's shivering Chihuahua growled back.

"I'm sorry," said Mr. Cheeseman. "She usually doesn't growl at other dogs."

"Yes," said Gerard from behind his father. "She usually only growls at sock puppets and bad people."

"This is my son Gerard. And this is Jough and Maggie."

Not about to be snubbed twice in one day, Steve cleared his throat.

"And this is Steve," said Mr. Cheeseman, completing the list. "Would you like to come in and sit down, Mrs. Frampton? I could put on some tea."

Pinky growled again and the Chihuahua growled back.

"Why, thank you," said Mrs. Frampton. "But perhaps that's not such a good idea considering that these two just don't seem to want to get along. I really just wanted to stop by and say welcome to the neighborhood and make sure you were getting settled in all right."

"Everything's just great," said Mr. Cheeseman.

"Well, that's wonderful. So tell me, what brings you all to our fair city?"

"We were just driving through and thought it looked like a very nice place to live," said Mr. Cheeseman. "And so far, we haven't been disappointed."

Pinky growled again and the Chihuahua growled back.

"That's an interesting looking dog you've got there," said Mrs. Frampton.

"She's a fox terrier," said Maggie.

"And not a very well behaved one at this moment," said Mr. Cheeseman as Pinky continued to growl at the Chihuahua. "Jough, would you take Pinky out of the room, please?"

"It's okay," said Mrs. Frampton. "I really should be going

anyway. I've got to get home and see to Mr. Frampton's supper. He can be very grumpy when he doesn't eat. Why don't I check back with you in a couple of days and see how you're doing?"

"That's very nice of you," said Mr. Cheeseman.

"Grrrr," said Pinky.

"Grrrr," said the Chihuahua right back.

Ethan and his children bid the woman good evening as she and her shivering, growling Chihuahua hurried off down the street.

"Well, how about that?" said Mr. Cheeseman. "How many towns these days have a neighborhood welcome committee? I told you I had a good feeling about this place."

"Well, the people sure seem friendly," said Jough.

"Yes," said Maggie. "Too bad the same can't be said of their dogs."

Meanwhile, a mere forty miles away, Pavel Dushenko was standing next to his small brown foreign car as a mechanic, familiar with such exotic makes, replaced the leaky radiator.

"Leon, please," said Pavel to his simian friend, who was still giving him the cold shoulder. Worse yet, the cold, hairy shoulder. "It was not Pavel's fault. I will soon buy for you a thousand feeshes. Tuna feesh, rock feesh, cat feesh, angel feesh, sword feesh, flying feesh. All the feeshes in ocean I will buy for you if only you forgive Pavel."

Before Leon could decide whether or not to forgive his friend, the sound of a ringing phone could be heard coming from inside the little brown car. Pavel reached in through the open window and pulled out a cell phone roughly the size of a small waffle iron. He extended a very long antenna and, with two hands, he flipped open the appliance-sized phone and put it to his ear. "Pavel here. Go ahead."

As Pavel listened to the caller, his left eyebrow slowly climbed higher on his forehead.

"And you are certain?" he asked. "You are certain it is them?" The longer Pavel listened the higher his eyebrow climbed and soon a sly smile spread across his face.

"Yes, that sounds like them. You have done well. Now you will keep close eye on them until time is right for Pavel and Leon to move in and take LVR."

Pavel snapped the large cell phone shut and turned to his pouting sidekick.

"We have them, my leetle minkey friend. And when time is right, we will pounce like hungry wolverines."

As Pavel smacked his fist into his palm for emphasis, a long black car was speeding down the highway a mere ten miles away. While Mr. 5 sat in the passenger seat, conducting a conversation on his tiny cell phone, the three other men in the car were deeply involved in a highly controversial discussion involving the differences between crumbling and crumpling.

"Okay, we're on our way," said Mr. 5 as he reinserted his matchbook-sized cell phone into his shirt pocket. He turned to Mr. 207. "Take a left at the next exit. Headquarters has just intercepted a cell phone call that sounds very interesting. Very interesting indeed."

It just so happened that the head office of a certain top secret government agency had also intercepted that same call and now Agents Aitch Dee and El Kyoo, international superspy Pavel Dushenko, and the henchmen from Plexiwave were all on their way to the little pink house on the quiet street in the quiet little town that was about to get a lot less quiet.

ADVICE ON THE DANGERS OF TECHNOLOGY

Why is it that we can put a man on the moon yet we can't seem to devise a more efficient, cleaner-burning engine than the one that put a man on the moon? The internal combustion engine, one of the greatest technological advancements in history, has an unfortunate downside, namely air pollution so thick that, very soon, sixty-four-packs of crayons will include the color Sky Brown.

With each technological breakthrough, it seems, we are the beneficiaries of untold advantages as well as the victims of considerable drawbacks. And no breakthrough provides us with more of both than a handy little device known as the telephone.

Before the arrival of the telephone, we had only the ability to speak to people who were actually there. For centuries, people had been searching for a means of communicating with people who were somewhere else. Early on, these people were called witches and were promptly set on fire. Later, they would be known as scientists.

The most noteworthy of these scientists was Alexander Graham Bell, who is credited with inventing the telephone in 1876. In the early morning hours of

March 10, he spoke those famous first words ever trans-
mitted by telephone.

"Mr. Watson, come here. I want you."

To which Watson replied, "I'll have to call you back,
I'm on the other line."

That day, the telephone became a reality. The jubi-
lant Mr. Bell immediately rushed off to the patent office
to patent what would prove to be the most lucrative
invention since some guy invented the patent.

Soon, Mr. Bell's phone was ringing off the hook with
orders for this fabulous new invention, which provides
us with the ability to pass on information in the blink
of an eye. And, as Mr. Cheeseman would soon find out,
this speedy delivery of infor-
mation can also be a terrible,
terrible drawback.

CHAPTER 22

Sunday came and managed to completely disregard its own name, choosing instead to be anything but a day of sun. In fact, it was very cloudy and unseasonably cool and looked as though it might very well rain. Still, Jough went off to his first baseball practice. Mr. Cheeseman began an attempt to hack into the computer's mainframe and write a new code for the LVR.

Gerard went to the secret spy fort in hopes that there might be intruders at whom he could throw a few dirt clods and Maggie took her bow and arrows and met Aurora out at the archery range for her very first lesson.

"Now this time try and aim at the target as you draw," said Maggie to her new student as Aurora locked her left arm, concentrated on the target, and drew the bow back.

"Good," said Maggie. "Now release."

Aurora released the string and, with a whisper, the arrow shot through the air.

"Yes," said Maggie. "You did it. Bull's-eye."

"I really did do it, didn't I?" said Aurora, her face beaming as she looked across the range at that arrow buried smack dab in the middle of those goat horns on Dean Greenfield's head. She and Maggie had affixed the painting to the target and Aurora's shot had managed to slice directly through Dean's newly painted unibrow.

"Wow," she said. "That felt really good."

"I told you it would," said Maggie.

"I'm so glad we met," said Aurora as she and Maggie walked toward the target to recover the arrows. "I think we're going to be very good friends."

"Yes," agreed Maggie. "I just hope we don't have to move away any time soon."

"Why would you move away? Don't you like this town?"

"Oh no," said Maggie. "I like it a lot. The people here are all very nice. Though I can't say much for their dogs. Mrs. Frampton's Chihuahua, for instance."

"Who's Mrs. Frampton?" asked Aurora.

"I thought you knew everyone in the neighborhood."

"I do," Aurora insisted.

"Well, apparently not, because Mrs. Frampton lives just down the street. She's head of the neighborhood welcome committee."

"I don't think so," said Aurora with a slight scoff that comes from knowing something someone else does not. "I should know because my mother is head of the neighborhood welcome committee. The only reason she hasn't been by to see you is because she's in Oregon visiting her sister."

"So if there's no one in the neighborhood named Mrs. Frampton," began Maggie slowly, "then who was that woman who came to our house yesterday?'

"Who knows?"

Then suddenly something hit Maggie that nearly knocked the breath out of her.

"Oh my goodness," she gasped. "Fraud, fraud, it's not the dog."

"What? Not the dog? What are you talking about?"

"The ghost. She was trying to tell me something."

"Ghost? What ghost?"

"The ghost at the bed-and-breakfast. She said it over and over again. 'Fraud, fraud, it's not the dog.' Pinky wasn't growling at the Chihuahua, she was growling at the woman. The woman who calls herself Mrs. Frampton."

Maggie turned to Aurora and took the much taller girl by the shoulders and looked her directly in the eye.

"I don't have time to explain but I need you to do something very important. I need you to go to the baseball practice field and get my brother. Tell him he needs to come home right away."

For a brief moment, Maggie thought of asking Aurora to bring her police captain father as well but quickly thought better of it. In a situation like this, no one could be trusted. Not even the police.

Maggie watched Aurora turn and run toward the baseball field as fast as her very long legs could carry her. She then turned and ran with her bow in hand toward the little pink rental house.

But, as it turns out, she would be too late.

Just thirty minutes earlier, Mr. Cheeseman had been hard at work, attempting to hack into the computer's mainframe, when the doorbell rang. He dropped what he was doing and answered the door to find the friendly faced Mrs. Frampton and her shivering Chihuahua on the front stoop. She was holding the dog in one arm and, in the other arm, a very decorative fruit basket.

"Sorry to bother you," she said. "But I just wanted to drop off this lovely welcome-to-the-neighborhood basket."

"Grrrrrr."

"Sorry," said Mr. Cheeseman. "I'll put her out back. Please come in and sit down."

Mr. Cheeseman scooped Pinky up abruptly and carried her off to the backyard. When he returned, he found the woman who called herself Mrs. Frampton standing in the living room, no longer holding her shivering Chihuahua, which had invited itself up onto the couch. The woman was now holding only the fruit basket. She was still smiling except that now the smile looked somewhat forced.

"Okay," said Mr. Cheeseman, failing to notice the difference in her countenance. "Would you like some iced tea or lemonade?"

"No thank you," replied Mrs. Frampton rather stiffly. "There is something else I would like instead."

"Oh. Okay. And what would that be?" asked Mr. Cheeseman as Pinky continued her barking and growling in the backyard.

The woman calling herself Mrs. Frampton reached into

the fruit basket, past the passion fruit and beneath the pomegranate and pulled out . . . a banana. She pointed it in Mr. Cheeseman's direction.

"I would like you to freeze and stay right where you are," she said, her smile altogether gone by now.

Mr. Cheeseman looked confused.

"I'm sorry, I'm afraid I don't understand. Is this some kind of joke?"

"This is not a joke, I'm afraid. And this is not a banana."

As if to prove her point, the woman cocked the banana-shaped gun with a menacing click, which caused Mr. Cheeseman to immediately lift his hands into the air.

"Now, now, Mrs. Frampton. I don't know what this is all about but I think you should put the banana down and leave peacefully before you get yourself into any more trouble than you already are."

"I will leave only when I have the LVR."

Mr. Cheeseman suddenly realized he had made a terrible mistake.

"So it wasn't your dog Pinky was barking at," he said. "It was you all along."

"Perhaps it was," said the woman, a smile returning to her face. She then reached up, grabbed her puffy white hair and yanked it from her head. She tossed the wig onto the couch next to her shivering Chihuahua, then shook out her shoulder-length blond hair. She removed her glasses and straightened her posture. She took hold of her long blue "old lady dress" with one hand and, with one quick motion, tore it away, revealing beneath it a short red "young lady dress."

She was, as it turns out, not an old woman at all but a rather attractive young woman with a rather unattractive— one might even say evil—smile.

Just then, the front door burst open and in walked Pavel and Leon, Pavel with his gun drawn.

"Aha! You have done well, Agent Kisa. Very well," said Pavel, circling the room slowly. "Pavel and Leon now will take over. When we are finished, I will tell headquarters of your excellent service to country."

"Thank you," said the woman in a low husky voice as she uncocked the bright yellow gun and put it back into the fruit basket. "It is an honor to meet the great Agent Dushenko."

"Please, call me Pavel," said the international superspy, trying hard to suck in his gut. "And this is Agent Leon."

Leon performed his highly elegant curtsy.

"And this is Agent Noodles," said Agent Kisa, pointing toward the Chihuahua, who had crawled beneath the white wig to try and get warm.

"They will write songs about you and your Agent Noodles," said Pavel.

"This is absurd," said Mr. Cheeseman. "You can take the LVR, but you'll never get it to work. Not without the code."

"Then you will give us code, too," said Pavel. "Or you will be shot."

"Well, I don't have the code, so I guess you'll have to shoot me."

"Be careful what you wish for," said Pavel, jabbing the gun in Mr. Cheeseman's direction as if it were a pointy stick.

Leon took no notice of this. He was busy wishing for something altogether different. Something nestled in the fruit basket on the table. He hadn't seen a banana of such a brilliant yellow since the outdoor markets of Khartoum. Hungrily, he reached for the banana and immediately attempted to peel it. By the time Pavel looked over at Leon, it was too late. Before he could yell or even open his mouth in preparation for yelling, the banana went off with a loud *crack*. The bullet sliced through the air and through Pavel's left thigh, causing him to drop his gun and fall to the ground.

"Ahhhhh!" he screamed, like someone who has just been shot with a gun shaped like a banana.

Leon looked at the smoking banana in his hand and realized what he had done. He dropped the gun and ran to Pavel's side.

"You idiot," said Agent Kisa, pushing Leon aside. "Look what you've done!"

As he watched his partner writhing on the ground, Leon suddenly forgot all about the fact that Pavel had been so willing to sacrifice his precious fish.

While Kisa and Leon tended to their fallen friend, Mr. Cheeseman eyed Pavel's gun lying on the floor just a few feet away.

"I can't believe I am shot by my own minkey," moaned Pavel as Agent Kisa began tearing her old lady dress into strips to use as a bandage.

Mr. Cheeseman took a step toward the gun, but his movement caught Leon's eye and the clever chimp reached out and tripped Mr. Cheeseman, who fell face-first to the floor. As Leon moved toward the gun, Mr. Cheeseman grabbed the only thing within his reach: the wig-covered Chihuahua named Noodles. He hurled the hairy blob at Leon, striking him in the chest and knocking him backward as Noodles tumbled across the room, still wrapped in the frost-white wig.

Mr. Cheeseman dove across the coffee table, landing next to Pavel's gun. He quickly grabbed the weapon and scrambled to his feet as Leon raised his hands above his head and Noodles stumbled out of the wig, quite dizzy and still shivering.

"All right," said Ethan. "Nobody move."

Nobody did move except for Pavel, who was still quivering with pain, and Noodles, who was still shivering involuntarily. Ethan backed slowly toward the phone and picked it up.

"What are you doing?" Kisa purred.

"What does it look like I'm doing? I'm calling the police. And an ambulance for your friend."

But when Ethan put his ear to the phone, he was surprised to find that there was no dial tone. He hit the button again, but the phone was still dead.

"I don't think you'll be calling anyone," came a voice from behind him. Ethan spun around as four strange men in black suits emerged from his kitchen. The man who spoke had remarkably hollow cheeks and a bald head that glistened with cold, clammy sweat. Ethan recognized another of the men, the one with a ring on each finger of his right hand, as the same man he and Olivia had found sitting in their living room two years ago, petting their dog and holding a suitcase containing two million dollars. This time, the man's massive hands held a coil of rope.

"Drop the gun, Mr. Cheeseman," said Mr. 5 as he and his three friends walked slowly into the living room.

"No," said Mr. Cheeseman, much to the surprise of the sweaty-headed Mr. 5.

"No? What do you mean, no?"

"I mean if you want the LVR, you're going to have to shoot me," said Ethan, practically daring them to do it.

As Mr. 5 looked quizzically at Ethan and wiped his sweaty forehead with his jacket sleeve, Gerard was just leaving the secret spy fort because, for the second day in a row, there were absolutely no intruders at whom to throw dirt clods and the boys decided to call it a day.

He walked across the field and noticed, parked in the driveway, a large white moving van, backed up to the garage. The vehicle didn't look too out of place, considering the number of times just such a van had pulled up to their various houses to deliver new furnishings. But what did look out of place was the long black car parked at the curb. Just the sight of that car almost caused Gerard to swallow the giant wad of flavorless bubble gum he'd been chewing for the past six weeks.

He broke into a run, down the street toward the house. He pulled two dirt clods from the pocket of his shorts and burst in through the front door, ready to fire upon any intruders who might be inside. Before he had a chance, however, he was grabbed by the enormous Mr. 29, who handled him so roughly that the dirt clods fell from his hands and the wad of gum popped from his mouth and hit the living room floor.

"Let me go," shouted Gerard. "Dad, what's going on?"

"It's okay, Gerard. Everything will be okay."

"That depends entirely on you, Mr. Cheeseman," said Mr. 5 as Pinky continued her barking from the backyard. "Maybe now you'd like to drop that gun."

Ethan relented and dropped his arm to his side and let the gun fall to the floor.

"Tie them up," said Mr. 5 to Mr. 29. "Then let's get that machine into the truck and off to the factory. And you," he said to Mr. 88, "do something about that barking dog."

"Got it," said Mr. 88 as he slid a cold black gun from beneath his jacket and walked toward the back door.

"No!" shouted Gerard. "Run, Pinky! Run and hide!"

Unfortunately, however, Pinky did not understand English and, as a result, kept barking every bit as loudly as before. Pinky did, however, understand fox terrier and it just so happened that Leon could speak it perfectly. He cupped his hairy hands around his big, wide monkey mouth and shouted in perfect fox terrier, "Run, Pinky. Run and hide. You're in great danger."

"Shut that monkey up this instant," snarled Mr. 5 as Mr. 88 walked out to the backyard, which was suddenly quiet. There was absolutely no sign of Pinky anywhere. Mr. 88 shrugged and walked back into the house. He had failed to see Pinky and her very pink skin standing perfectly still in front of the pink lilacs that grew up against the fence.

"Must have run away," said Mr. 88 as Mr. 207 had almost finished tying Ethan's and Gerard's hands behind their backs.

"Fine," said Mr. 5. "Now let's get that machine into the van."

As they struggled to load the oblong, mirror-covered LVR into the large white van, the sun was finally starting to come out over the baseball diamond where Chief Codgill and his Police Pals were taking batting practice with Jough on the pitcher's mound.

Meanwhile, Aurora's long legs were carrying her as fast as they could toward the practice field. When she got there, she saw a baseball field full of teenage boys. Since she had never met Jough, she wasn't sure to whom she should deliver her message and so she ran to her father.

"Which . . . one's . . . Jough?" she said, her lungs searching for more air.

"What? What's wrong?" asked Chief Codgill.

"Jough," she repeated. "Which one's Jough?"

"He's pitching," said Chief Codgill. "Now do you mind telling me what this is . . . ?"

Aurora took off running toward the pitcher's mound and shouted Jough's name just as he released the ball. The batter swung and the ball jumped off the bat with a resounding crunch and struck a half second later with a thud, also of the resounding variety. It hit Aurora right between the shoulder blades.

213

She toppled face-first onto the ground as Chief Codgill ran from the dugout toward his fallen daughter. He rolled the girl onto her back and sat her up partway. The ball had completely knocked the wind out of her. The rest of the Police Pals gathered round, not sure what to say or do.

"Back off," said Chief Codgill, his baby-butt chin jutting outward. "Give her some room. Are you okay, Aurora?"

Still without enough air in her lungs to speak, Aurora looked up and pointed at Jough.

"What is it?" said Chief Codgill.

Finally, Aurora managed to speak but only one syllable at a time, which made her sound not at all unlike Tarzan. "Jough," she said, gasping. "Must go . . . home. Go . . . quick . . . ly. Trou . . . ble. Magg . . . ie . . . sent . . . me."

"Sorry, Coach," said Jough, "but it sounds like I need to get home right away."

"Maybe I should go with you," said Chief Codgill.

"No," said Jough, distrustful of even his own coach and captain of the local police force. "You should stay here and make sure she's okay. It's probably nothing serious. I'll see you tomorrow."

Chief Codgill, the rest of the Police Pals, and the tall, pretty girl named Aurora all watched as Jough took off running at top speed in the direction of the little pink house.

With her bow still in hand, Maggie ran up the street toward the house, her legs aching from having run so far and so fast. She was still half a block away when she saw a large white moving van pulling out of the driveway and onto the street, heading away from her. A familiar-looking black car with black tinted windows pulled out from the curb and followed the van.

With absolutely no chance of catching them, Maggie stopped running. She pulled an arrow from her quiver and loaded it into the bow. She dropped to one knee, drew the bow back, and took careful aim. She released the arrow and, like a comet, it screeched through the air toward the rear tire of the long black car and entered with a sharp hiss.

Though the direct hit did not cause a blowout as Maggie had hoped, it would mean a slow leak in the tire, which meant they wouldn't get too far before having to pull over.

Maggie ran the remaining half block to the house. The first thing she noticed was that the garage door was open and the LVR was gone. She ran into the house and took in the scene before her. Furniture was upended, a fruit basket and a white wig lay on the floor, and a young blond woman, a monkey, and a shivering Chihuahua were trying to drag a man with a bleeding leg toward the front door.

"Where is he?" she demanded, her bow at the ready should she need it. "Where's my father?"

"He is not here," groaned Pavel. "He was taken by other men. Men with guns. You must not look for him. Is too dangerous for leetle girl."

"Shut up," said Maggie. "Where did they go?"

"I do not know," said Pavel. "They said take LVR to factory."

"Factory," said Maggie slowly but her train of thought

was interrupted by the sound of Pinky barking and scratching at the back door. She ran to the kitchen as Pavel's friends continued to try and drag him out the front door and toward the little brown car parked at the curb. When Maggie opened the kitchen door, Pinky practically jumped into her arms. "Pinky, are you okay?"

Pinky licked Maggie's face for a solid minute before remembering that the house had been full of intruders. She growled and ran to the front door just as the little brown car drove off down the street, right past Jough, who was finishing his full-on sprint to the house.

He ran inside and practically collided with Maggie.

"What's going on?"

"They were here. They took Dad and the LVR."

Jough pounded his fist against the wall.

"Darn it!"

Not satisfied, Jough made an attempt to kick the wall, too, but he found his left foot stuck to the floor. With a yank, he pried it loose, then reached down and peeled a large wad of pink bubble gum from the sole of his shoe.

"Looks like they got Gerard, too."

"We've got to get help. We have to call the police," said Maggie, trying her best to remain calm.

Jough suddenly felt dizzy and the palms of his hands were moist with perspiration. He was about to sit down on the floor when he remembered the promise he made to himself just a few weeks ago. The next time he found himself in a dangerous situation, he would be a man of action, just like his father.

"No," said Jough. "We're not going to call the police. I don't trust them. But you're right. We do need help."

Maggie watched as Jough ran off to his bedroom and returned a moment later holding a small piece of paper. It was a business card for Captain Jibby's Traveling Circus Sideshow.

"But they were on their way to Hollywood. Who knows where they might be by now."

"It's worth a shot," said Jough, picking up the phone, which he discovered had no dial tone. "They must have cut the phone lines. Come on."

With Pinky behind them, Jough and his sister ran down the street to the large green house. Inside the house, someone was practicing the bass drum. Jough pounded loudly on the door, trying not to pound in rhythm with the drum, to ensure being heard. The drumming stopped and a moment later Elliot, bass drum mallets in hand, opened the door.

"Jough. Is practice over already?" said Elliot, surprised to see his client standing on the doorstep. "I hope Chief Codgill isn't being too soft on you guys. As your agent, I must say it's of the utmost importance that you maintain peak conditioning."

"Our phone's out," said Jough. "I've got to borrow yours if you don't mind."

"Well, I don't know," said Elliot. "My dad's not home, so I'm not supposed to have anyone in."

"It's an emergency," said Maggie.

Elliot still looked hesitant. "You don't know my dad. He gets pretty angry when I break the rules."

"Well, could you bring the phone out here?" asked Jough.

"Great idea," said Elliot with a sense of relief. "I suppose that would be permissible under the circumstances."

Elliot disappeared into the house and Jough, Maggie, and Pinky waited for what seemed like a lifetime for him to return with a phone. Jough grabbed it greedily and punched in the numbers on the business card as fast as his fingers would let him.

"It's not long-distance, is it?" asked Elliot. "I'm not allowed to make long-distance calls."

Jough ignored Elliot because he was too busy counting the rings in his head. *One. Come on, answer. Two. Pick up the phone, Jibby. Three. Please be there.* After the fourth ring, Jough heard a recording of Jibby's voice.

"Captain Jibby speaking. I'm not here right now and that's all I'm going to say without my attorney. Ha-ha. So leave a message and, if I like you, maybe I'll call back."

"Jibby, it's Jough. Ethan's son." Jough tried to remain calm so as not to speak too quickly and slur his words. "Listen, you said if we ever needed anything, we should call you right away. Well, we need your help. My father and my brother have been kidnapped."

Jough went on to tell Jibby's recorded voice the exact location of the little pink house in their quiet little town and that his father and brother had been taken to a factory.

"I'm not sure where the factory is," said Jough.

"Wait a minute," said Maggie. "Aurora told me they're building a new factory out on Canyon Road. A factory that's going to make microwave ovens."

"Sounds like a possibility," said Jough, who continued with his message. "We think the factory may be out on Canyon Road. Please, if you get this message, hurry. The lives of our dad and our brother may depend on it."

Jough hung up and handed the phone back to Elliot.

"Your father's been kidnapped?" gasped Elliot. "And your brother? By whom?"

"I'll tell you later," said Jough. "Right now, we've got to get out to that factory."

"But how?" said Elliot. "Canyon Road is five or six miles from here."

"Well then," said Jough, "I guess we'll have to drive."

"Drive?" Elliot exclaimed. "But you're fourteen years old. You can't drive."

"I'm fourteen and a half and, yes, I can drive," said Jough. "My dad taught me for emergency purposes, and this is definitely an emergency."

"Grrrr."

Pinky was looking back toward the little pink house, where a sporty red car had just pulled into the driveway. Aitch Dee and El Kyoo stepped out and walked to the front door, their guns drawn.

"Were those . . . guns those crooks were holding?" asked Elliot, his voice trembling.

"Well, they weren't bananas," said Jough. "And those are no crooks. They're coats. Probably CIA."

"CIA? What kind of trouble are you guys in?"

"The worst kind you can imagine," said Jough.

Just then a police car drove slowly down the street and

stopped in front of the pink house. The door opened and out hopped Chief/Coach Codgill. Cautiously, he walked carefully up the walkway toward the open front door.

"How are we going to get to the car now?" asked Maggie.

"We're not," said Jough, looking to Elliot's driveway at the beautiful, perfectly restored deep blue 1957 ragtop convertible. "We're going to borrow that one."

"What?" shrieked Elliot, practically falling over. "Are you crazy? My dad will freak out if he knows I let you borrow the phone. Now you want to borrow his car?"

"As your client, your only client, I must insist that it's of the utmost importance that you let us borrow that car," said Jough, looking right into Elliot's terrified eyes.

ADVICE ON SAFE DRIVING

We the people love our automobiles. Driving is every bit as American as apple pie, though, statistically speaking, driving is far more dangerous than pie. (With the possible exception of rusty nail/scorpion pie. Delicious but dangerous.)

To give you an idea as to the precarious nature of driving, may I point out that each year the number of people killed in auto accidents is greater than the number of people killed in both world wars—and those people were driving tanks.

The best way to avoid an accident is to increase your knowledge of the rules of the road. I have therefore compiled the following quiz to help you on the road to safer driving. I advise that you study it closely.

1. When changing lanes you should:
   - A) Check your mirror and proceed when safe.
   - B) Check your mirror and your blind spot and proceed when safe.
   - C) Drift over until you hear glass.

2. A red eight-sided sign always means:

    A) Stop.

    B) Go.

    C) Danger! Red octagons ahead!

3. Your seat belt should always be worn:

    A) Over your shoulder and across your lap.

    B) Under your shoulder and between your legs.

    C) With slacks and a sporty top.

4. You should loan your father's convertible to your fourteen-year-old neighbor:

    A) Never.

    B) Only in an emergency situation.

    C) Only when it is absolutely essential to the story.

CHAPTER 23

Coral Bjornsen had just left her bed-and-breakfast and was buzzing down the sidewalk on her way to the bingo parlor when a car sped by, driving right through a massive puddle, completely dousing the woman in cold, muddy water.

"Oh, spackle!"

"You just splashed that woman," said Elliot from the backseat as his father's convertible raced toward the edge of town. "And I wish you would slow down."

"Look at it this way," said Jough. "The faster I drive, the sooner we'll have the car back. Now how do we get to Canyon Road?"

"Turn left here," said Elliot with just enough warning for Jough to make a hairpin turn, the tires chirping as they tried their best to hang on to the pavement.

No sooner had they made the left turn than Pinky let out a growl.

"We must be getting closer," said Maggie. "Good girl, Pinky."

As Elliot directed them closer and closer to the factory, Pinky's growls became more consistent until she was growling practically nonstop.

There were no houses on Canyon Road, or much of anything else for that matter. It was just a long stretch of road winding through a steep canyon with sagebrush, wildflowers, and tall grass sprouting up on either side.

"There it is," said Maggie, pointing up ahead. "The factory."

A large building with a flat roof and several smokestacks, the factory stood at the end of the road, sitting in the middle of a large dirt lot surrounded by a tall chain-link fence. Next to the factory was an enormous warehouse that must have been the size of an airplane hangar. Painted on the warehouse, above the giant door, was a bright blue letter *P* made up of wavy lines.

"Plexiwave," said Maggie. "We'd better be careful. These guys are bad news."

Just outside the warehouse, a large man dressed in a black suit was busy changing the rear tire on a long black car with tinted windows.

Jough stopped the car about a hundred feet from the factory behind a stand of tall weeds. Being seen would take away the only weapon they had, the element of surprise.

"They must be in the warehouse," said Jough. "All we have to do is get past one guy."

"One guy?" said Elliot. "I don't know if you've noticed, but that one guy is the size of a grizzly bear."

"The bigger they are, the harder they fall," said Jough

as he quietly opened the door of the convertible. "Okay, Elliot. You stay here with Pinky. We'll be right back."

"You'd better be," said Elliot. "My dad gets home at four and, when he does, his car better be waiting for him."

Jough and Maggie crawled along the road behind the tall-growing weeds, toward the factory. When they got to the chain-link fence, Jough motioned to Maggie to wait there. Peering over the weeds that grew up around the fence, Jough could see the enormous Mr. 29 with his back to them as he squatted down in front of the car to tighten the lug nuts on the spare tire.

Jough found a nearly round rock, about the same weight as a baseball, only smaller. He picked the rock up and stuffed it into his pocket, then, as quietly as he could, began climbing the fence, inching slowly and breathlessly toward the top. When he had gotten just over halfway, he lost his footing and nearly fell, causing the fence to rattle noisily.

Mr. 29 stopped what he was doing and craned his neck around as far as he could. Luckily, it was not far enough that he could see Jough clinging to the fence, scarcely daring to breathe. Mr. 29 decided it was nothing and went back to tightening the lug nuts as Jough continued his painfully slow climb to the top of the fence.

When he reached the top, he swung both legs over and landed hard on the other side of the fence. His less-than-stealthy landing caused Mr. 29 to stand up and whirl around, which is exactly what Jough wanted him to do, for when he turned around Jough removed the round rock from his pocket and gripped it as he would a baseball. Mr. 29

watched with puzzlement as Jough went into his windup and tossed a screwball in his direction.

As the rock sailed toward him, Mr. 29 did not move. He did not move because it was quite obvious the rock was not going to hit him. At the last moment, however, the pitch broke sharply to the right and, before he could react, it caught Mr. 29 right between the eyes. The big man did indeed fall hard as he crumpled to the ground, unconscious.

"Nice pitch," whispered Maggie.

"Screwball. Now come on, let's go."

Maggie scrambled up the fence quickly and dropped down next to Jough.

"What do we do now?" she asked.

"I have an idea," said Jough.

In the middle of the brightly lit, otherwise empty warehouse, was the white moving van and, next to it, the large, egg-shaped disco ball known as the LVR, completely assembled and ready to go. All it needed in order to be completely operational was the computer code, which, at that precise moment, Mr. 5 was trying to persuade Mr. Cheeseman to give to him. And the way he was trying to persuade him was by twisting his left earlobe in a counterclockwise direction to the point that, if it actually were a clock, by now it would be yesterday.

Mr. Cheeseman screamed and nearly fell out of the chair on which he'd been propped up.

"Okay, I will ask you again," sneered Mr. 5, his sweaty face very close to Ethan's. "What . . . is . . . the . . . code?"

"I told you," said Ethan. "I only have half of it. The other half . . ."

"Is missing. Yes, you keep insisting that's the truth, and I believe it now as much as the first time you told me."

Gerard, meanwhile, was sitting against the cold steel wall on the smooth concrete floor with an old handkerchief tied tightly around his mouth. His ankles and wrists were bound with rope. All he could do was sit and listen as his father moaned in agony.

Mr. 5 released Mr. Cheeseman's now-purple earlobe and nodded to Mr. 88, who reached into his pocket and produced a syringe filled with a bright blue fluid.

"This," said Mr. 5, taking the syringe, "is CR70, otherwise known as True Blue. It's the absolute latest in truth serum, of which I personally oversaw the development. You needn't worry. It's harmless, really. Just make sure you don't operate any heavy machinery for the next couple of years."

Mr. 5 held the syringe up to the light and, with a flick of his forefinger, tapped out a couple of tiny air bubbles. As he did, Ethan saw something strange in the reflection of Mr. 5's sunglasses. Something that made him very angry. It was the tattoo on Mr. 5's wrist, which, when reflected in his glasses, read *Plexiwave*.

"You," said Mr. Cheeseman. "You're Dr. Fiverson."

"I'm afraid I don't know what you're talking about," said Mr. 5.

"You killed my wife."

"Well, if you're certain of that," said Mr. 5, "then you know I will stop at nothing to get what I want."

As Mr. 88 rolled up Ethan's sleeve and prepared him for the injection of True Blue, Gerard decided he had had quite enough of sitting by and doing nothing. Despite the fact that his hands were tied tightly behind his back, he found he was able to sneak two fingers of his non-sock-puppet hand into his back pocket. And with those two fingers, he was able to grasp one lucky Indian arrowhead. One very sharp, lucky Indian arrowhead.

Being careful not to drop it, he gently pulled the ancient artifact from his pocket and, as Steve helped out by holding it tightly in his mouth, began sawing at the rope around his wrists.

"Just relax now, Mr. Cheeseman. In a few seconds you will find yourself confessing to things you've completely forgotten about." Mr. 5 moved the needle toward Ethan's exposed forearm. Outside the warehouse, a car horn honked twice.

"Well, it's about time," said Mr. 5. "Let him in."

Gerard worked the arrowhead frantically as Mr. 88 walked to the large double doors. Gerard sawed faster and the arrowhead slipped and caught his finger. The sting was enough to make Gerard want to cry out but he fought off the urge and continued his sawing. The blood from his finger made the arrowhead sticky in his hand and easier to grip. He renewed his attack on the rope and finally the arrowhead completely severed the rope and Gerard was able to wriggle his hands free and remove the rope around his ankles. Quickly and without any unnecessary motion he reached into his back pocket and removed his reserve supply of bubble gum, which he was at no time without.

Keeping his eyes fixed on Mr. 5, Gerard silently unwrapped the gum, then removed the handkerchief from his mouth and shoved the entire package into his mouth. His well-practiced jaws fought against the stiffness of the gum but it was taking too long. Mr. 88 had reached the double doors. He pressed a red button on the wall, causing the doors to fold slowly inward.

The long black car with tinted windows was idling just outside the entrance. Inside it, Jough's right foot was poised over the gas pedal, twitching slightly in anticipation.

"Are you sure about this?" asked Maggie.

"Piece of cake," said Jough. "But just in case, hold on!"

Jough's foot came down hard on the gas pedal and the car screeched forward, pinning Maggie against the back of her seat.

"What on earth is that idiot doing?" said Mr. 5.

The car sped right toward Mr. 207, forcing him to dive to the ground to avoid being run over. The car skidded to a halt right next to Mr. 5, who, by now, was voicing his displeasure with Mr. 29's driving abilities with words that you might commonly find written in spray paint on a condemned building.

As Mr. 5 continued to curse and yell, the driver's-side door flew open, knocking Mr. 5 backward to the ground. He screamed in pain, then rolled over and pulled the hypodermic needle from his thigh.

"Uh-oh."

Jough and Maggie jumped out of the car and ran to their father. Mr. 88 stood in shock, like someone who has taken a bite of what he thought was chocolate ice cream but was actually liver paté. He fully expected to see Mr. 29 emerge from the car, not Jough and Maggie.

He pulled his gun and ran toward them. He was halfway there when Gerard removed the wad of gum from his mouth and tossed it into the path of the sprinting gunman. The gum hit the floor just as Mr. 88's shoe clamped down on it and, when it was time for that shoe to leave the floor again so Mr. 88 could continue running, the pink goo held it in place just long enough to send Mr. 88 belly-flopping onto the smooth, hard concrete. The air left his lungs like someone popping an inflated paper sack and his gun skimmed across the slick surface of the floor like a hockey puck.

Mr. Cheeseman, his hands still tied behind his back, was being helped into the backseat of the car by Jough and Maggie when Gerard ran toward them.

"There's Gerard," said Jough. "Come on, get in!"

Gerard tumbled into the backseat with his father while Jough and Maggie scrambled into the front.

"Good work, Gerard," said Maggie.

"It's all because of my lucky arrowhead," said Gerard, proudly displaying the sharp and bloodied stone before turning his attention to his father's tied hands. As he began to carve away at the knots with the arrowhead, Jough hit the gas, snapping Gerard's head back as the car lurched forward.

"Hey!" said Steve. "Take it easy."

It would soon be apparent to Steve and everyone else in the car that Jough had no intention of taking it anything close to easy. He hit the brakes and sliced the wheel sharply to the left just as he had seen his father do. The car spun around a complete 180 degrees to face the open door of the warehouse.

"Nice move, Jough," said Mr. Cheeseman.

No time to reply, Jough leveled all his weight on the gas pedal and the car screeched toward daylight.

"Shut that door!" screamed Mr. 5, climbing to his feet. "I steal forks from restaurants! Ahhhh!" Mr. 5 smacked himself in the temple, trying to knock the potent dose of True Blue from his brain.

Mr. 88 got to his feet and ran toward the red button on the wall, his shoes slipping desperately on the smooth concrete.

"Hurry, Jough," yelled Maggie as Mr. 88 smacked the button on the wall and the large doors began to close. The beam of sunshine from the outside world grew smaller and smaller as the car sped toward the shrinking exit.

"We're not going to make it!" screamed Gerard.

Maggie hid her face in her hands. Gerard hugged Steve tightly. Mr. Cheeseman winced and prepared for the worst. Jough grit his teeth and pushed harder on the gas pedal, even though it couldn't possibly go any farther without breaking through the floor of the car.

The front of the long black car shot through the narrowing exit just as the large heavy doors came together, sandwiching the back of the car with the grotesque sound of metal being crushed, crumpled, squished, mashed, smashed, smooshed, and pulverized. The car came to a sudden and violent stop, though its wheels continued to turn.

Jough kept pressing on the gas pedal but the car was firmly in the grasp of the heavy steel doors and the tires just spun on the concrete floor, giving off a terrible noise and a noxious black smoke.

"Everybody out!" yelled Jough in his take-charge voice. The doors flew open and everyone piled out. "This way."

Jough ran toward the chain-link fence and the others followed. They leaped over Mr. 29, still lying unconscious, a baseball-sized lump on his forehead. Gerard had not had time to free Mr. Cheeseman's hands, and he struggled to keep up.

"After them!" bellowed Mr. 5, bulging blue and red veins making his bald head look like a road map. "I like warm milk and cookies at bedtime!"

With the car blocking the exit, Mr. 88 and Mr. 207 had to climb over it to get out of the warehouse. This gave Jough and the others a much-needed head start. Jough's original plan had been to drive the car up next to the fence, climb on top of it, and jump easily to the other side. Without the car to stand on, getting everyone over the fence in time would be far more difficult.

Jough reached the fence first and immediately dropped to the ground on all fours, offering the small of his back as a step for the others.

"Go!" he shouted to Maggie as she ran up to the fence.

"Youngest first," she said, waiting for her little brother to catch up. Gerard used his brother's back as a launch pad, leaping halfway up the fence with some help from his sister. An excellent climber of all things (trees, fences, large mounds of dirt), Gerard had no trouble reaching the top of the fence and, in just seconds, had dropped down on the other side.

"Hurry, Dad!" cried Maggie to Mr. Cheeseman, who wondered how he was going to climb the fence without the use of his hands, which were not yet completely untied.

"You two go ahead," said Mr. Cheeseman. "I'll be okay."

"We're not leaving without you," said Jough, rising to his feet.

"It looks like none of us are going anywhere," said Mr. Cheeseman as Mr. 88 and Mr. 207 ran toward them and Mr. 5 climbed over the car and out of the warehouse.

"Gerard," said Mr. Cheeseman, turning to his younger son. "Go for help. It's our only chance. Run as fast as you can, and don't stop for anything."

"But . . ."

"But nothing. Just go!"

Gerard spun around, put his spiky head down, and ran up the road. This certainly did not escape the notice of Mr. 5, who shouted, "He's getting away, you idiots. Shoot him. I'm wearing Spider-Man underpants!"

Mr. 207 stopped running and fished his gun from his shoulder holster. In all his years of taking orders from Mr. 5, never before had he been told to shoot at a child. The prospect of doing so made him very nervous. Not because his conscience bothered him in any way, but because children were generally smaller than grown-ups and, thus, much harder to hit. Without further hesitation, he leveled his gun at Gerard and fired. The bullet hit the chain-link fence and shattered in two, both fragments landing in the dirt at Gerard's desperately moving feet. As Mr. 207 took aim once more, Gerard disappeared behind the tall weeds.

"Don't just stand there," yelled Mr. 5. "Go after him! My real name is Milton Cornelius Flowers!"

Mr. 207 ran for the fence as Mr. 88 ran up and grabbed Jough and Maggie by the napes of their necks, squeezing hard enough to send a shooting pain right down their spines.

"Let them go," said Mr. Cheeseman. "Let them go and I'll give you the code. You have my word."

"No, Dad, don't do it," shouted Jough as loudly as one can while the back of his neck is being crushed.

"Shut up," said Mr. 5 as he grabbed Ethan's well-tied hands and forced him to the ground with a knee in his back. "I intentionally speed through school zones!"

A hundred feet away, from the relative safety of the ragtop convertible, Pinky growled and barked and Elliot watched in horror and amazement as Gerard ran toward them while Mr. 207 reholstered his gun and began climbing the fence.

"Oh no," said Elliot to himself. "This is not good. This is not good at all."

For the record, Elliot was exactly right. The situation was

very dire indeed. Suddenly, he heard a low rumbling behind him that grew louder and louder until finally he could ignore it no longer. He looked out the rear window of the convertible and what he saw both confused and frightened him. It was coming toward him so fast. Much too fast. Perhaps a hundred miles an hour or more.

As the big black bus raced closer and closer, he could see the man behind the wheel. The man seemed to be screaming, his white teeth standing out in stark contrast to his bushy, pumpkin-colored beard. As it turns out, the man not only appeared to be screaming, he actually was screaming.

As Captain Jibby gripped the steering wheel so tightly his fingers lost their natural coloring, he screamed at the top of his lungs, "Rammming speeeed!"

The convertible nearly blew over onto its side as the bus roared by, missing it by mere inches. Gerard stopped running and watched as the bus raced toward the chain-link fence, not slowing one bit.

"Go, Jibby!" shouted Gerard, who had never in his life been happier to see a school bus.

Jough, Maggie, and Mr. Cheeseman saw the bus too and undoubtedly shared in Gerard's happiness.

It goes without saying that Mr. 5 was not the least bit happy to see the bus, nor was Mr. 88. But it is quite certain that the person least happy to see that particular school bus was Mr. 207, who had climbed roughly two-thirds the way up the chain-link fence when he saw the bus coming toward him at one hundred miles an hour, otherwise known as ramming speed.

Before he could react, the bus crashed into the fence with such force that the very posts that held it upright were torn out of the ground. Mr. 207 was thrown through the air like a rag doll, though it should be noted that he completely lacked any endearing doll-like qualities. He might very well have been killed had he not landed directly on top of the still-unconscious Mr. 29 as the bus blasted through the fence, sending pieces of it flying through the air like shrapnel.

Mr. 5 and Mr. 88 could only stand and stare as the bus lurched to a stop amid a cloud of dust. When it finally cleared they could see Captain Jibby and his band of sideshow misfits: Three-Eyed Jake, Dizzy, Aristotle, Sammy, and Juanita. By the way she gripped the large wooden rolling pin in her right hand, it was apparent that Juanita had no intention of using it to make cookies.

"Release the children," Jibby bellowed as the others fanned out alongside him. "Or prepare to meet your maker."

"Stand back," said Mr. 5 as he pushed Ethan farther into the dirt. "Stand back or my associate will break the children's little necks. I would love to learn to play the pan flute!"

Mr. 88 ignored the pan flute comment and squeezed harder on the children's necks, almost causing Jough and Maggie to lose consciousness.

"I told you once before," said Jibby, "that if you ever threatened me again, it would be the last time."

Then, as calmly as one can, considering the circumstances, and without taking his eyes off Mr. 88, Jibby pulled out the knife blade on his Swiss Army hand. Then he pulled out the can opener, the hole puncher, the scissors, and the corkscrew. When the Swiss Army knife's entire arsenal had been snapped into the ready position, Jibby grasped the handle with his left hand and began unscrewing it until the whole thing was no longer attached his wrist.

"I'm lactose intolerant!" said Mr. 5 right before smacking himself in the temple once more. "Now I'm warning you. Drop the knife!"

Jibby did drop the knife as Mr. 5 instructed but probably not in the exact way Mr. 5 had hoped that he would. Instead of lowering his arm and dropping the knife directly to the ground, Jibby chose instead to raise his arm high above his head and quickly "drop" the knife in a sharp, horizontal direction right toward Mr. 88. The knife's many tools whistled through the air as it turned end over end until the scissors pierced Mr. 88's shoulder.

Mr. 88 screamed in a pitch so high that only dogs could hear it. Pinky growled at the ear-piercing howl and Mr. 88 released his grip on the two small necks he'd been squeezing and stumbled backward. He reached up to pull the scissors from his shoulder but instead stabbed himself with the protruding corkscrew, causing him to let out another falsetto scream.

"Run!" yelled Mr. Cheeseman to his two children.

"Yes, over here!" said Jibby.

But neither Jough nor Maggie could persuade their feet to move in the direction of the black school bus. Without so much as a word or a glance between them, the two had each come to the exact same decision at the exact same time. They would run as their father had instructed, but they would not run away. Their fear quickly turning to anger, they lowered their heads and ran toward Mr. 5 and Mr. 88, growling like ravenous wolverines.

"Get 'em!" snarled Maggie in a voice so vociferous she almost scared herself.

"I collect commemorative plates!" yelled Mr. 5 before releasing Mr. Cheeseman and scrambling over the wreckage of the fence, away from the angry children. Mr. 88 followed but his pant leg caught on the wire fence and, for the second time that day, his bruised rib cage hit the ground, knocking the wind from his lungs.

Jough and Maggie ran to their father and began untying his hands.

"That was a very foolish thing to do," said Mr. Cheeseman. "I told you to run."

"You didn't say in which direction," said Jough, pulling the rope away from Mr. Cheeseman's wrists.

"Look!" With his newly freed hand, Mr. Cheeseman pointed in the direction of Mr. 5, who was racing up the hill toward the convertible.

"Sammy," said Jibby. "You know what to do."

"Aye aye, Captain."

The man with the strength of two and a half men bent at the knees and picked up one of the steel fenceposts that had been yanked out of the ground. He took the exceedingly heavy pole at one end and proceeded to twirl around, faster and faster, much like a washing machine on the spin cycle. When he could spin no faster, Sammy let go of the pole, sending it sailing and twirling through the air like a helicopter blade.

Mr. 5 did not see the pole coming toward him, but he did hear it whooshing through the air just seconds before it clipped his legs out from under him, sending him sprawling to the dusty ground and badly fracturing his left leg.

Three-Eyed Jake and Aristotle ran over to Mr. 88 and pulled him to his feet before he could even think about making an escape.

"We got him, Captain," said Jake.

"Good work, men." Jibby walked toward the trembling Mr. 88. "I'll take that," he said as he pulled the Swiss Army knife from Mr. 88's shoulder, causing the man to once again warble like a soprano. Jibby wiped the scissors clean on his blue buttoned sleeve.

"Okay," he shouted. "Let's get these scalawags tied up and put in the bus."

Sammy, Dizzy, Aristotle, and Juanita went to work tying up Mr. 29, Mr. 88, and Mr. 207.

"Thank goodness," said Mr. Cheeseman. "Thank goodness you showed up when you did. How did you find us?"

"Luckily I check my messages regularly," said Jibby, screwing the Swiss Army knife back onto his right wrist. "Your boy called me. We just happened to be in the area."

"Yes, I guess that was lucky," said Ethan.

"Well, it wasn't all luck," said Three-Eyed Jake with a friendly punch to Aristotle's shoulder. "We were in the area because Ari here remembered a vision he had had several years ago."

"Crystal clear," said Aristotle. Then he smiled and blew a large pink bubble.

"Well, I must admit," said Mr. Cheeseman, "I'm quite amazed by your psychic abilities. Now if you can just tell us where we might find Gerard."

Mr. Cheeseman needn't have worried as Gerard was just up the road, watching while Mr. 5 wriggled about on the ground, gripping his fractured femur.

In a moment, Elliot and Pinky appeared at his side.

"You must be Jough's little brother," said Elliot.

"And you must be Elliot," said Gerard.

"I sure am," said Elliot. "And I don't know what's going on here, but I've never seen anything like it. I mean, did you see that guy with the steel pole? He must have thrown it a mile."

"That's Sammy," said Gerard. "He has the strength of two and a half men."

"You don't say," mused Elliot. "I wonder if he has an agent."

Looking down the road, Gerard saw his father, his brother, and his sister running toward him. Ethan swooped down on his son and grabbed him in a hug so tight the boy's spine made a slight cracking noise. Then Jough and Maggie took turns hugging their little brother.

"I was afraid you'd been shot," said Maggie.

"I guess I'm faster than a bullet," said Gerard.

"Me too," said Steve.

This time Pinky did not growl at Steve but only because she was, at that very moment, busy displaying her complete and utter lack of fondness for Mr. 5 by tugging and tearing at his pant leg.

"Get him, Pinky," said Gerard.

"Who is that guy?" asked Elliot.

"He's the guy who killed our mother," said Jough with both anger and sadness in his voice.

"Get him, Pinky," said Elliot.

"Ahhhh! Get that animal off me," screamed Mr. 5, clutching his injured leg. "I drink milk directly from the carton and put it back into the fridge!"

"Grrrrrr."

"Okay, Pinky, that's enough," said Mr. Cheeseman. "We'll need him in one piece when the police show up and arrest him for murder."

For a moment, Ethan wasn't quite sure he meant what he had just said. Part of him wanted to see Pinky tear to pieces the man who had taken the love of his life, the man who had caused him and his family so much pain. He even thought about doing it himself, but before he could act on his impulse, he noticed Jibby, Aristotle, and Three-Eyed Jake standing next to him.

"Don't worry, Ethan," said Jibby, his hand on Mr. Cheeseman's shoulder. "We'll make sure he gets what he deserves."

"I know. Thanks."

"I sometimes bite my toenails!" Mr. 5 revealed.

"Get this no-good toenail biter out of here," said Jibby to Aristotle and Three-Eyed Jake. "Put him with the others."

With little regard for the man's badly damaged leg, Aristotle and Three-Eyed Jake each took an arm and dragged Mr. 5 back toward the bus, ignoring his frequent outbursts of agony and bizarre confessions.

"Cheer up, Dad," said Maggie. "We won. We got them before they got us."

"Yes," said Mr. Cheeseman with a weak smile. "You're right."

But Ethan did not feel much like celebrating. Sure, Mr. 5 and his Plexiwave compatriots had been captured, and Pavel Dushenko had been left helpless with a gunshot wound to the leg, but the coats were still hot on their trail, and that meant only one thing. Just by looking at her father's face, Maggie knew exactly what that one thing was.

"So I guess we have to move away again," she said.

"I'm afraid so," said Mr. Cheeseman. "Our cover's been blown. Until the LVR is up and running, we've got no choice but to keep moving."

The news fell heavily on the ears of his three children, who, in the short time they'd lived in their new town, had come to like it very much. But now Gerard would have to relinquish his membership in the secret spy fort, Maggie would have to say good-bye to her new friend and art teacher, Aurora, and Jough would have to, once again, put his baseball career on hold.

"Can we at least go back home and get our stuff?" asked Jough.

"That won't be possible," said Mr. Cheeseman. "We don't know who might be waiting for us. This time we'll have to leave with nothing but our good health and just be thankful we've still got that."

"But how can we leave without my dirt clod collection?" said Gerard.

"And how can we leave without my baseball glove?" said Jough.

"More importantly," said Maggie, "how can we leave without a car?"

"There's a large white moving van in that warehouse that no one seems to be using. And enough room in back that I won't have to disassemble the LVR this time. I can load it up in one piece."

"Where will you go?" asked Jake.

"I don't know," said Mr. Cheeseman. "Another town in another part of the country."

"Will you ever come back?" Elliot asked Jough, who turned to his father.

"I don't know. Dad? Will we?"

"It's hard to say. Anything's possible." This seemed to be Mr. Cheeseman's way of saying that it was most unlikely that they would ever come back.

After an awkward silence during which everyone studied the distant horizon or the tops of their shoes, Elliot stepped toward Jough, his right hand extended.

"Well, good luck, Jough. It was very nice meeting you."

"Same here," said Jough. "If I ever make it to the major leagues, I'll give you a call."

"I'd appreciate that," said Elliot.

"It's the least I could do," said Jough. "If you hadn't let us borrow your dad's car, who knows what might have happened."

"All right," said Ethan. "Let's get the LVR loaded up and ready to go before the wrong people show up here."

"No!" said Gerard, angrily stabbing at the ground with his foot. "I'm not leaving without my dirt clods!"

"We've got no choice, Gerard," said Mr. Cheeseman. "I'm sorry."

"You're always sorry," squeaked Steve. "And I'm sick of it."

"Grrrr," Pinky growled at the sock puppet.

It was at that moment that Steve decided he had had just about enough of being growled at by a hairless fox terrier.

"You be quiet," he squeaked, moving in close to Pinky's snarling face for emphasis. "I'm tired of you growling at me all the time."

And it was at that moment that Pinky decided she had had just about enough of a snarky, one-eyed sock puppet squeaking so loudly and so closely to her face. And so, she reached out with her snarling teeth and bit Steve firmly on the area that would have been reserved for his nose if he indeed had a nose.

Gerard screamed as Pinky tore the sock puppet from his hand.

"No, Pinky! No!"

At this point, Pinky was beyond listening. With her nails and teeth, she tore and ripped at the helpless sock puppet as Gerard could only watch in horror.

It took mere seconds to complete her murderous act. Pinky then walked over to Gerard and gently licked his newly exposed left hand.

"Get away," said Gerard angrily. "Get away from me. Look what she did. She killed Steve."

Everyone was indeed looking at what remained of Steve. They were looking in shock and amazement because, amid that pile of torn-up yarn and thread was a small mint green piece of paper.

"Dad?" said Jough, scarcely able to breathe.

"I see it," said Mr. Cheeseman.

He moved toward it slowly, as if any sudden movement might frighten it away. The children watched as their father lowered himself to one knee and picked up the piece of paper, which had been folded down the middle. Slowly, he unfolded the paper and, when he read what had been written on it, he broke down and sobbed right there in the middle of that dusty lot, his tears forming mud on the ground beneath him.

Without looking up, Mr. Cheeseman handed the piece of paper to Jough, who took it and studied it.

"What?" said Maggie impatiently. "What does it say?"

"It says," Jough began, choking back a large lump in his throat. "It says, *don't be afraid, be amazing.*"

Mr. Cheeseman wiped his eyes with the sleeve of his

shirt and stood up. He reached into his back pocket and removed the other half of the mint green paper and gave it to Jough, who positioned the two halves side by side and read aloud.

"When danger lurks and your heart is racing, don't be afraid, be amazing."

The code, as Maggie had originally suspected, had been ciphered as a bit of wisdom from their mother and was just the kind of advice they might have expected from the woman who saw so much in them.

Smiling as he hadn't in years, Mr. Cheeseman gathered his children in his arms. "You kids *were* amazing today," he said. "In fact, you've been amazing throughout this whole ordeal. But today? Today was something else. Gerard?" Mr. Cheeseman roughed up Gerard's spiky head. "I think that was probably the most heroic use of bubble gum in the whole entire history of bubble gum."

Gerard smiled and Mr. Cheeseman turned to Maggie. "And Maggie . . . those archery lessons turned out to be the best money I ever spent. That was a heck of a shot."

"But how did you . . . ?"

"I saw you from the back window of the car. Incredible shot. Absolutely incredible." It was Maggie's turn to smile and Mr. Cheeseman smiled back, then put his hand on Jough's shoulder.

"Jough?"

"Yes, Dad?"

"That was, without a doubt, the best getaway driving I have ever seen."

"Thanks," said Jough, feeling like a real man of action. "It was nothing, really."

"It was something. Your mother would have been very proud of you three."

Gerard cleared his throat. Mr. Cheeseman looked down at his youngest child, then followed the boy's gaze to the ragged tatters of yarn that had once been Steve, lying in the dirt. "Sorry, Gerard. You're right."

Mr. Cheeseman crouched next to Gerard and gently scooped what was left of the one-eyed sock puppet into his hands. "Your friend Steve gave his life today to save that of another. Your mother would have been very proud of you all."

"You mean she *will* be very proud of us," said Jough, holding up the two pieces of paper.

"Yes," said Mr. Cheeseman with a quiet smile. "She will be very proud of you."

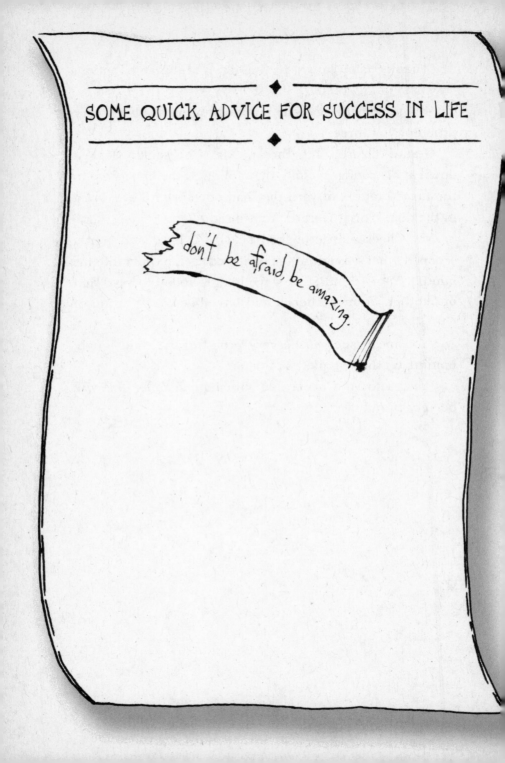

SOME QUICK ADVICE FOR SUCCESS IN LIFE

don't be afraid, be amazing.

CHAPTER 24

According to Gerard, it was Steve's wish that, in the event of his demise, he be cremated, his ashes scattered in the wind and recommitted to the earth. And so, as his surviving friends and relatives gathered in the warehouse parking lot, near the old black school bus, Captain Jibby volunteered to say a few words.

"As the captain of a seafaring vessel," he said, "I am fully authorized to perform weddings, funerals, and minor surgery." He flipped open the knife on his Swiss Army hand for effect.

"I thought you were the captain of a school bus," said Maggie.

"Yes, I suppose I am," he said, snapping the knife back. "But I was once the captain of a ship. A very long time ago."

"I don't mean to be insensitive," said Mr. Cheeseman, "but I think we need to do this quickly. We've really got to get moving."

"And I need to get my dad's car home before he freaks out," said Elliot.

249

"Right," said Jibby. "On with it then." Jibby bowed his head and the others did likewise. "Dearly beloved, we are gathered here today to honor a great soul. Steve was a sock of strong fiber and great bravery. A sock who died in the service of friends and family, for which there is no more noble a cause. May he rest in peace and may his spirit live on in our hearts forever."

Jibby nodded to Dizzy, who struck a match and lit the small pile of twigs and dry grass on which lay the deceased. He then turned and nodded to Juanita, who walked forward and handed him his fiddle.

Jibby placed the instrument beneath his bright, over-grown chin and began to play a sad but beautiful melody. Slowly, the flames grew and consumed Steve's remains. As the fire finally died out, so did the music, leaving nothing to the ear but the wind whistling through the tall grass and the gentle sniffing of noses.

"That was beautiful," said Mr. Cheeseman with a sniff of his own.

"I call it 'Requiem for a Sock Puppet,' " said Jibby.

"Thank you. For everything. I wish there was some way we could repay you for all you've done."

"Actually," said Jibby, "now that you mention it, there is a favor I'd like to ask of you."

"Anything," said Mr. Cheeseman. "Anything at all."

"I was wondering if you might give us a ride."

"A ride? But you've got your bus and . . ."

"No," said Jibby. "I mean I was wondering if you might give us a ride . . . in the time machine."

For a moment, Mr. Cheeseman was at a complete loss for words.

"You mean the dime machine," Jough quickly interjected.

"No, I mean the time machine. We've known about it for quite some . . . well, for quite some time."

"Okay," said Mr. Cheeseman, willing to drop the charade. "Who are you then? CIA? KGB?"

"Actually," said Three-Eyed Jake, "we're privateers."

"What's a privateer?" asked Gerard.

"A privateer," said Mr. Cheeseman in a very serious tone, "is a pirate."

Upon hearing this, one thing immediately crossed the minds of Jough, Maggie, and Gerard. Pirates steal things. Had it been a mistake to trust Captain Jibby? Had it been his intention all along to steal the LVR? Were his hearty laugh and pleasing personality merely a facade? Deep down, were he and his friends no better than Plexiwave and its agents of evil?

"You're pirates?" said Elliot with a roll of his eyes. "Pardon my skepticism, but everyone knows there are no pirates around here."

"True enough," said Three-Eyed Jake, taking a step in Elliot's direction. "But we're not from around here."

Elliot took a step back and suddenly wished he had kept his thoughts to himself.

"Well, if you're not from around here, then where are you from?" asked Gerard.

Three-Eyed Jake turned to Captain Jibby, looking for

permission to answer the question. Jibby nodded ever so slightly, and Jake went on. "We're from a place very far away," he said. "A little place called 1668."

This wasn't much of an answer as far as Mr. Cheeseman and his children were concerned. This answer only resulted in more questions.

"Sixteen sixty-eight?" Gerard repeated. "But which street?"

"No, no lad. It's not an address," said Jibby. "It's a time. The year 1668, that's where we're from."

As the words left his mouth, a tension seemed to leave Jibby's body. It appeared that keeping that bit of information a secret had been weighing on him for some time.

"I don't understand," said Maggie, considering the possibility that Jibby was either lying or completely insane. "If you're from 1668, how did you end up here?"

"It's all part of the curse," Three-Eyed Jake said in an intense, whispery kind of voice. "The curse of the White Gold Chalice."

"What's a chalice?" asked Gerard.

"It's a cup," said Maggie.

"I beg your pardon, young lady," said Jibby, "but the White Gold Chalice is more than just a cup. For centuries it was used by Danish kings and is said to have been passed down from the mighty hand of Odin himself."

"Okay," said Mr. Cheeseman, wanting desperately to believe. "But that doesn't explain how you all ended up here."

"Oh, but it does," said Jibby. "It explains everything. Because the White Gold Chalice, you see, is said to carry a terrible curse that afflicts anyone who wrongfully possesses it, which, in this case, would be us."

Jibby untied a small leather pouch attached to his belt. From the pouch he removed what looked like a trophy, the kind that might be presented to the winner of a horse race, a golf tournament, or a pie-eating contest. It was a cup, silver in color with a fluted lip and strange symbols molded along its base.

"So then . . . you stole it?" said Jough.

"Foolish, I know," said Jibby, looking somewhat ashamed. It should be noted that shame is not an emotion one normally associates with pirates. This, along with the fact that Pinky was curled up at Jibby's feet, helped put Mr. Cheeseman at ease.

"Stealing is never a good idea," Jibby continued, looking at his reflection in the polished surface of the cup. "Neither is tempting fate, for no sooner had we taken the chalice than a hellish storm circled about our ship. The mighty *Bella Juanita* was struck by lightning no fewer than a dozen times."

"You were struck by lightning?" gasped Maggie.

"Aye," said Jibby with an involuntary shudder. Three-Eyed Jake and the rest of Jibby's crew also shuddered.

"Does it hurt to get struck by lightning?" said Gerard.

"Well, it doesn't help," said Jibby, the smile returning to his face.

"So that's how you ended up here?" asked Jough, every bit as skeptical as his friend Elliot but too polite to come right out with it.

"It would seem to be the case," said Jibby. "Transported through time on a wickedly powerful bolt of electricity."

Jough turned to his father. "Dad? Is that even possible?"

"Scientifically speaking, electromagnetic kinesis has never been ruled out as a possibility. So it certainly could be true."

"Oh, it's true all right," said Jibby. "Or my name isn't Gentleman Jibby Lodbrok."

This bit of information caused Jough to look at Maggie and the both of them to look at their father.

"Lodbrok?" said Ethan. "That's my wife's maiden name."

"Olivia," said Jibby. "She would be our great-great-great-great-granddaughter if I'm not mistaken."

"Our?" asked Maggie.

"Juanita and me. Say hello to your great-great-great-great-great-grandmother."

Juanita moved to her husband's side and he placed his non–Swiss Army hand on her shoulder.

"You mean," Gerard began excitedly, "that we're the dentists of pirates?"

"I think you mean we're the descendants of pirates," Maggie corrected her brother.

"Ex-pirates," Jibby corrected Maggie. "We've given up our thieving ways once and for all, which wasn't easy. After all, it's in my blood. My own roots can be traced back to Ragnor Lodbrok, the great Viking raider of the eighth century."

"Wait a minute," said Gerard. "You mean we're the descendants of pirates *and* Vikings? I don't believe it. This is the greatest thing that's ever happened to me."

Everyone laughed, which made Gerard quite pleased with himself, as it wasn't always easy to make grown-ups laugh.

"Pardon me for saying so, Jibby," said Ethan, "but the whole thing sounds quite fantastic."

"Yes," agreed Jibby. "It does. And so does a machine resembling a disco ball that can travel through time. But I believe with every bone in my body that it is also true, because my good man Aristotle saw it in a vision and led us to you, or you to us. And I believe you folks are the only ones who can help us to go back in time, to that fateful day in 1668 before we stole the chalice. It's the only way to break the curse that has plagued us and our descendants all these years."

"Hold on," said Jough with annoyance. "You mean all this bad stuff has happened to us because you stole that chalice?"

"I'm afraid so," said Jibby. "And for that, I apologize and beseech your forgiveness."

Jough's expression softened, and Maggie smiled. "It's okay, Jibby," she said. "You're our friend, and friends always forgive one another."

"Thank you. So what do you say, then? Will you take us with you? If we're able to lift the curse, I'm sure things will go a lot easier for you."

"I don't know," said Mr. Cheeseman. "I'm not sure the machine's big enough for all of us. Besides, it's never been tested. It works in theory, but scientifically speaking, who knows what might happen?"

"There's only one way to find out," said Jough.

"You're right, Jough," said Ethan. "There's only one way to find out."

A rumbling noise echoed through the empty warehouse as Mr. Cheeseman hoisted up the back door of the white cargo van to reveal the LVR, fully assembled and awaiting entry of the computer code he hoped would turn it from a giant oblong disco ball into a fully functioning time machine.

"Magnificent," said Aristotle at first sight of the LVR. "Just as she appeared in my vision."

"She's a beauty, all right," Jibby agreed. "A finer ship I've yet to see."

"Well," said Ethan, climbing into the cargo hold of the van. "Let's see if she works as good as she looks."

"Do we need to take it out of the truck first?" asked Jough.

"Shouldn't matter," said Mr. Cheeseman. "Either way, our first order of business is to enter the code. Should take just a second to decipher the other half."

Mr. Cheeseman removed a pencil from his shirt pocket, then took the mint green piece of paper that had been hidden inside Steve. Quickly, he scribbled a number beneath each letter on the paper. When he had finished, he looked it over carefully.

"There," he said. "That should do it. We're ready to enter the code into the computer. And Jough?"

"Yes, Dad?"

"I'd like to extend that honor to you."

Jough suddenly felt more like an adult than he ever had before. "Thanks, Dad. But don't you think . . . ?" Jough nodded in the direction of his little brother.

"Yes," said Maggie. "I think Steve would have wanted it that way."

"You're right," said Mr. Cheeseman. "Gerard? Would you like to enter the code?"

The thought of being responsible for something of such importance made Gerard both very proud and very nervous. "But . . . what if I make a mistake?"

"Then we'll all be blown to smithereens," said Maggie with a horrified look.

"Is that true, Dad?" said Gerard doubtfully.

"It's not true," said Mr. Cheeseman. "But I feel as if we're running out of time here. So don't make a mistake."

Gerard looked at the van, not sure how he was expected to get his short body up and into the cargo hold.

"Allow me," said Sammy, stepping forward. With one hand he easily lifted the boy up next to his father.

"Thanks, Sammy," said Mr. Cheeseman. "Oh, and Jibby?"

"Aye, sir," said Jibby with a quick salute.

"If you don't mind, I'll be needing a screwdriver."

Jibby removed his hand and, well, handed it to Mr. Cheeseman, who pulled out the screwdriver and used it to remove a small panel on the side of the LVR. Beneath the panel was a keypad.

"I'll read out the numbers," Mr. Cheeseman said to Gerard. "And you enter them here. Got it?"

"Got it."

As Mr. Cheeseman read out the numbers, each corresponding to a letter in the note, Gerard carefully punched those numbers into the computer.

"That's it," said Mr. Cheeseman when the final number had been entered. "Now let's keep our fingers crossed. See that switch, Gerard?"

Next to the keypad was a small red switch. Written beneath it was the word *Power*. "Hit it," said Mr. Cheeseman.

Gerard took a deep breath and moved his finger slowly toward the switch. Maggie and Jough could scarcely bear to watch. After all, this was it. Should the LVR fail to work, they would most likely never see their mother alive again.

Jibby and his crew had their own reasons for being nervous. This was likely their only chance to break the curse that had plagued the Lodbrok bloodline for centuries.

Gerard's finger reached the switch. He paused for a moment and looked at his father.

"It's okay. Go ahead."

Gerard flipped the switch, but nothing happened. For two agonizing seconds, absolutely nothing happened. And then, a low hum and a greenish blue light shot out from beneath the LVR. The frequency of the hum and the intensity of the light grew until everything and everyone in the warehouse was bathed in a rich, turquoise glow.

"We did it!" exclaimed Maggie. "We really did it!" Without thinking, she turned and gave her big brother an enormous hug. Captain Jibby hugged Juanita. Gerard hugged Ethan. Three-Eyed Jake removed his bandanna and tossed it triumphantly into the air. Dizzy removed his special ear-muffs and tossed them as well, then promptly toppled over; Sammy caught him before his head struck the concrete floor.

"I knew it would work," said Jough. "I knew it all along."

Ethan looked at the LVR and nodded slowly. "It runs," he said. "Whether it works or not remains to be seen."

CHAPTER 25

"I'm sorry, but the monkey will have to wait here," said the plump young nurse.

Leon watched as she pushed Pavel's wheelchair across the waiting room floor.

"Don't worry, my leetle minkey friend," the international superspy called out. "Everything will be good and also not bad."

Agent Kisa followed the nurse, her sharp heels clacking across the tile floor, her purse vibrating with the shivering Agent Noodles hidden inside. Leon wished the purse were big enough for him as well but, for now, he would have to remain in the waiting room. Luckily there was something in the waiting room that caught Leon's attention and kept him busy until Pavel returned.

Much to Leon's relief, the wound to Pavel's leg turned out to be only superficial and the doctor was able to stop the bleeding with a mere thirteen, sorry . . . fourteen stitches, before sending Pavel and his friends on their way. The last anyone saw of them, they were driving toward the airport in their little brown car with Pavel at the wheel, Kisa and her shivering Chihuahua in the passenger seat, and Leon in back.

"Did I not tell you, Leon?" said Pavel. "Did I not tell you that Pavel would get for you many beautiful leetle feeshes for you to love for all time?"

Leon's little fuzzy face lit up as he watched the many colorful tropical fish nip at the flakes of food floating on the surface of the enormous fifty-gallon tank.

"Sure, they will not have big parade for us and maybe not write songs about us and maybe throw us in prison for many years for not getting LVR, but you will have your leetle feeshes to be making you very happy."

Leon smiled and gave the box of fish food another tap.

When the doctor at the clinic walked out to his waiting room at the end of the day and noticed the aquarium was missing, he immediately phoned the police. At that very moment, however, Police Chief Roy Codgill could not be bothered with such minor crimes. Along with government agents Aitch Dee and El Kyoo, he was on his way to a factory on the outskirts of town.

Driving down the dusty road, the first thing he saw was a blue ragtop convertible parked at the side of the road. As he and the government agents continued to the warehouse they saw aspiring sports agent and bass drummer Elliot Walsingham sitting on the back bumper of a black-and-white school bus.

"Good afternoon, Coach," said Elliot as Chief Codgill

climbed out of his police cruiser, Agents El Kyoo and Aitch Dee right behind him. "How may I help you today?"

"We're looking for your client," said Chief Codgill. "Where is he?"

"I'm not sure exactly. And that's the truth."

"What in heaven's name is that?" said Aitch Dee, looking at the school bus.

"It says *Captain Jibby's Traveling Circus Sideshow*," said El Kyoo.

"I can read, thank you," said Aitch Dee.

"They're inside," whispered Elliot out of the corner of his mouth.

"Who's inside?" said Chief Codgill.

"The men who poisoned Jough's mother. Don't worry. They're tied up. See?"

Elliot reached out and pulled the door open to reveal four men dressed in black, their hands and legs tied tightly just as he had reported.

"I'm fond of easy listening music," said Mr. 5 with no prompting whatsoever. "I also enjoy decorative soaps and wearing ladies' hats."

"What are you talking about?" demanded Aitch Dee. "Where's Ethan Cheeseman?"

"And where's Jough Psmythe?" added Chief Codgill.

"The truth is," said Mr. 5, "I don't know. But the last time I saw them they were heading toward the warehouse. To the LVR."

"What the heck is an LVR?" asked Chief Codgill.

"I'm afraid that's top secret," said Aitch Dee.

Mr. 5 yelled out, "The LVR is a time—"

Aitch Dee quickly slammed the metal door closed.

"He's obviously suffered a severe head injury. Keep these criminals covered while we search the warehouse."

Slowly, Aitch Dee and El Kyoo crept toward the warehouse, where the long black car still sat, squished, squashed, and crushed between the heavy steel doors.

"What are we going to do when we find them?" whispered El Kyoo.

"We're going to arrest them, of course," said Aitch Dee.

"On what charge?"

"We'll make something up later. Right now, our only concern is making sure the LVR is in the control of our top secret agency within the United States government."

As quietly as they could, Aitch Dee and El Kyoo climbed over the crumpled car and into the warehouse, where they found a white moving van.

While Aitch Dee kept his gun trained on the van's cargo door, El Kyoo called out, his voice ricocheting off the steel walls and the concrete floor.

"Mr. Cheeseman? Can you hear me? It's okay, you can come out now. Everything's gonna be all right. We're here to help you."

The two agents waited for a moment, but nothing happened.

El Kyoo inched closer to the van and, while Aitch Dee kept his gun trained on the van's cargo door, El Kyoo slid it up, revealing what was inside, which amounted to approximately two thousand cubic feet of oxygen and nothing else. The van was completely empty.

Nowhere in the warehouse was there any sign of Ethan, Jough, Maggie, Gerard, a psychic, hairless fox terrier, or any member of a certain traveling circus sideshow. It appeared that they had disappeared without a trace. In fact, without so much as a trace of a trace.

Also in a state of extreme disappearedness was the LVR. It was simply nowhere in sight, for at that moment the giant, oblong disco ball was soaring along the Time Arc, its occupants on their way to undo what had been done. To reverse the curse of the White Gold Chalice and to save the life of Olivia, Mr. Cheeseman's kind and beautiful wife and mother to his three smart, attractive, polite, and relatively odor-free children.

But that, my friends, is a whole nother story.

Before becoming an author and advisor,
DR. CUTHBERT SOUP
held many other fun and rewarding
jobs. For a brief time he worked at the
mall as a smoke detector but was
eventually replaced by a machine. A
talented musician, he then moved to
New York City and landed a gig playing
elevator music. He was fired, however,
when his trombone kept smacking other
people in the elevator. Currently the
founder and president of the National
Center for Unsolicited Advice, Dr. Soup
resides in a semisecret location with
his dog, Kevin, and his two pet snails,
Gooey and Squishy. In his spare time he
enjoys cajoling, sneering, and practicing
the trombone in crowded areas. This is
his first book.

www.awholenotherbook.com

Before Gerard could announce his new name to the world, Mr. Cheeseman emerged from the LVR with the freshly extracted dashboard compass in hand. "Got it," he said, the autumn leaves crunching beneath his feet as he dropped to the ground. He handed Jibby his Swiss Army knife and Jibby expertly screwed it back on. "How's Dizzy making out?"

Like a slow, smooth elevator, all eyes moved up the giant cottonwood looking for Dizzy, who was nowhere to be seen but could be heard scrambling from branch to branch about three-quarters of the way up the tree. "Well, he hasn't fallen yet," said Jibby, leaning back against the LVR. "That's a good sign."

"It sure is," said Rat Face Roy.

Mr. Cheeseman gasped and recoiled at first sight of Gerard's new friend. "Ahh! Get that thing away from me," he said, jumping behind his twelve-year-old daughter.

"Relax, Dad," said Jough. "It's just Gerard's new sock puppet."

"Oh," said Ethan, panting heavily and feeling rather foolish. "For a second there I thought it was a rat." Though you would think, as a scientist, he would be used to working with rats, Mr. Cheeseman was deathly afraid of them and thus happy to learn that the creature before him was merely an old sock with pink bubble-gum eyes.

"So what's your friend's name, Gerard?" asked Mr. Cheeseman, trying to regain both his composure and his dignity.

"His name's Rat Face Roy. But my name's not Gerard anymore."

"It's not?" said Mr. Cheeseman. "Did I miss something?"

"We've decided it's time to change our names," said Jough.

"Oh?" Mr. Cheeseman seemed somewhat surprised, even though the whole name-changing thing had been his idea to begin with. "So you really think it's necessary this time, considering the circumstances?"

"That's what I said," Maggie agreed. "But I was outvoted."

"Democracy in action," said Mr. Cheeseman. "That's what made this country great."

"Well," said Jough, "if it really is 1668, America doesn't exist as a country yet."

"True enough, Jough."

"Actually, my new name is Chip. Chip Krypton," said Chip, who had previously gone by such names as Don Von St. John, Rory McJagger, Gary Indiana, and, of course, Jough Psmythe.

"Chip Krypton," Mr. Cheeseman repeated. "Has a nice ring to it."

"Thanks."

"How about you, Maggie?" asked Mr. Cheeseman. "What should I call you from this moment forward?"

"Well, I've narrowed it down to two, but I think I'm going with Penelope Nickelton. You can call me Penny for short," said Penny, who, in the past, had answered to such names as Shari Chablis, Brooke Babblestone, Calliope Plume, and, most recently, Magenta-Jean Jurgenson, or Maggie for short.

Mr. Cheeseman thought for a moment, running the name over and over in his head. "Penny Nickelton. It's both complimentary and contradictory, depending on how you look at it."

"Exactly," said Penny with a satisfied smile.

Gerard had originally wanted to go first but now was happy that, in his opinion anyway, the best had been saved for last.

"My new name is the bestest of all," said Gerard proudly.

"It's the best of all," said Penny.

"But you haven't even heard it yet," said Gerard, who, before, had given himself such names as Luke Tuna, Po Ming, Chance Showers, and, just a couple of weeks ago, Gerard LaFontaine. "My new name is . . ."

Gerard paused for dramatic effect, as he always did.

" . . . Captain Fabulous!" Gerard extended his arms out in front of him and performed a quick fly-around, complete with Mach 5 sound effects, before coming in for a forceful landing as if he were about to face off against an army of giant robots.

Captain Jibby laughed and shook his head in disbelief. Juanita snorted and slapped her knee. Three-Eyed Jake treated Gerard to an exaggerated salute. Gerard saluted right back then took flight once more while declaring loudly, "Captain Fabulous and his trusty sidekick, Rat Face Roy, will save the world from evil villains everywhere."

"Uh, I don't think so," said Penny.

"What do you mean?" asked the confused superhero when he had touched down once more.

"What I mean is there is absolutely no way on earth I am going to refer to you as Captain Fabulous."

"Why not?"

"Yeah, why not?" said Rat Face Roy.

"For the same reason you wouldn't want to call me Queen of the Universe."

"Well," Mr. Cheeseman interjected. "Perhaps there's an easy solution to this. Maybe Captain Fabulous has an alter ego."

"What's an alter ego?" asked Gerard.

"It's a superhero's true but secret identity," said Chip. "You know, the way that Superman is really Clark Kent."

"Superman is really Clark Kent?"

"It's pretty obvious," said Penny, "to everyone but you and Lois Lane."

"Okay," Gerard conceded. "Captain Fabulous's alter ego will be . . . Teddy Roosevelt."

Penny scoffed so hard she almost lost her balance. Sometimes she wondered if her little brother did things with the express purpose of annoying her. "What? You can't name yourself after one of our most famous presidents. People will think you're crazy."

"Not people in 1668," said Teddy. "In 1668, he hasn't even been borned yet. Has he, Dad?"

"Uh, no," said Mr. Cheeseman. "He hasn't been . . . borned."

"Someday, when he is, people will think he was named after me," said Teddy.

"I think it's disrespectful and in poor taste," said Penny.

"I don't know," said Chip. "Somehow, I think the other Teddy Roosevelt would have approved."

A shrill sound interrupted the controversy and all eyes shot to the sky, where Dizzy was standing near the very top of the cottonwood tree, waving his arm wildly and whistling loudly.

"Smoke!" yelled Dizzy. "I see smoke!"

Off in the distance, a good five miles away, a single pillar of thin gray smoke was angling into the breezy, pale blue October sky.

🕐

"There, that should do it," said Mr. Cheeseman as he, Jibby, and Sammy lowered the ceiling panel back onto the

LVR. "As long as it doesn't rain, we should be okay." For the next thirty minutes or so, everyone was put to work gathering leaves and branches, which were used to completely cover the LVR until it looked like nothing more than a large, egg-shaped mound of brush.

"Let's hope nobody finds this," said Chip, adding one last branch for good measure.

"That might cause quite a panic," said Mr. Cheeseman, who had actually had much bigger concerns on his mind. Would he be able to repair a very modern machine with only spare parts that could be found or manufactured in 1668? Had he doomed them all to spend the rest of their lives in a time without electricity, indoor plumbing, bubble gum, and doughnuts? Would he ever again see his beautiful wife again? Would his children once again be able to hug the mother they loved so dearly? Though these questions weighed heavily upon him, he cleverly hid the fear and doubt in his heart by decorating his face with a confident smile.

And so, manning the compass, the doubtful, smiling scientist led the group through the dense forest, in the direction Dizzy had pointed. Along the way, he jotted down notes on their exact position so that once they were able to secure the materials they needed to fix the LVR, they would actually have a means of finding it again.

"Are you sure this is the past?" asked Teddy. "It doesn't look very old-timey around here. It just looks sharp and stickery."

Several hundred years later, the land beneath their feet

would be home to a large housing development, two car dealerships, and an enormous supermall featuring no fewer than three coffee shops and a place selling deep-fried cheese. But, for now, the ground on which they traveled had, perhaps, never before been trodden upon by human beings and the going was not easy, especially for those of diminutive stature, like young Teddy. Rat Face Roy snagged himself several times on the thick bramble bushes and once had to be carved out of his predicament by Jibby's knife. As a result, he was beginning to look a bit tattered, and Teddy was beginning to feel a bit exasperated. If there was any doubt before, this confirmed that being small is a very bad idea.

"Are we almost there?" he whined. "I'm hungry. And my feet hurt."

"Well, maybe you should turn into Captain Fabulous," said Penny. "Then you could fly to the nearest town and get something to eat."

"Hey, could you bring me back a burger and fries, Captain Fabulous?" said Chip. "And a strawberry shake if you don't mind." Penny laughed.

"Stop making fun of me," Teddy insisted.

With a sigh, Mr. Cheeseman stopped and turned toward the squabble. "Chip. Penny. That's not helpful right now."

"Okay," they both said.

Sammy took a knee next to Teddy. "Would you like a ride?" he asked.

"What about your bad back, Sammy?" Penny asked the strong man.

"Ah, it's all right. How much could he weigh? He's not the size of tuppence." Sammy hoisted Teddy onto his shoulders, then, with a plaintive wail, stood up, causing Teddy's head to smack into a low hanging branch.

"Ow!"

"Sorry," said Sammy, stepping aside. "How's that?"

"Well, my feet don't hurt anymore," said Teddy, rubbing his head.

"It's the bloody curse," said Jake, narrowing his one remaining eye.

"Or it could have been a simple accident," Mr. Cheeseman suggested.

Aristotle stepped forward, his eyes dancing wildly beneath the shadow of his bushy eyebrows. "There are no such things as accidents," he said in a dramatic, whispery voice. "Everything happens for a reason."

"I don't understand this curse business, anyway," said Chip. "I mean, how did it all get started anyway?"

Jibby stroked his beard and drew in a deep breath. "Well," he said, "if you really want to know . . . "

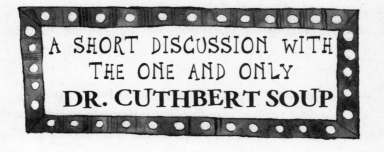

A SHORT DISCUSSION WITH THE ONE AND ONLY DR. CUTHBERT SOUP

How did you meet the Cheesemans?
I first met a very young Ethan Cheeseman when we both attended Southwestern North Dakota State University. While I was working toward my doctorate, he was just a wide-eyed freshman. I advised him to let me take him under my wing. Shortly thereafter, he advised me to start using deodorant.

Were you a particularly odorous child?
I much prefer the term "odorific."

What is your least favorite smell?
I have many, as I have an extremely keen sense of smell. In fact, I once worked at the mall as a smoke detector before being replaced by a machine. If I had to pick one, I would say that I have always hated the smell of burning money. I must find a more agreeable way of heating my mansion this winter.

What, or who, inspired you to tell the Cheesemans' story?

I was inspired to tell the story by my dog, Kevin, who needed money for an operation, which I am happy to say was a fabulous success and he has never looked younger.

Why the fear of intermittent windshield wipers?

They always manage to pause just long enough for you to forget they're there. Then, when you least expect it, they jump up in front of your face, scaring the daylights out of you. Ten seconds later, you find yourself reliving the horror all over again. I am also afraid of toasters for similar reasons.

Does the Cheeseman family like cheese? If so, what's their favorite type?

I am unaware as to whether the Cheeseman family has a particular penchant for cheese. I can, however, confirm the rumor that the Roosevelt family is very fond of . . . rooses.

What is your favorite kind of pie?

Unfortunately, my doctor has advised me to avoid all circular foods.

CAN'T GET ENOUGH OF
A WHOLE NOTHER STORY?
CHECK OUT

www.AWHOLENOTHERBOOK.com

Watch videos
about Dr. Soup
and his books.

Read another sneak peek from *Another Whole Nother Story.*

Read the FAQ with Dr. Cuthbert Soup. He answers lots more
questions . . . even though he's pretty sure FAQ stands for
Fuzzy Aardvark Quintuplets.

Use the New Identity Customizer. It's great for
when you're on the run from corporate villains,
government agents, or international superspies!

And so much more!

Unsolicited Writing Advice

**Isn't it time you told a Whole Nother Story of your own?
Find out how with Dr. Soup's unsolicited writing advice:**

You'll laugh, you'll cry, you'll be an author before you know it!

Of the many subjects you will learn in school, the most important are said to be the Three Rs: reading, riting, and rithmetic. As you may have noticed, rspelling did not make the list.

Of these so-called Three Rs, riting can often be the most difficult. Seriously, when was the last time you heard about someone suffering from mathematician's cramp? Or reader's block?—"I've been staring at the bookshelf for hours and I can't think of anything to read!"

Because riting can sometimes be challenging, I've decided to offer some unsolicited advice on the subject. To start you on your way to more enjoyable riting, simply go to **www.awholenotherbook.com**. Every couple of weeks, you will find a new exercise designed to make the process of riting easy, exciting, and efun, also known as the Three Es.

Good luck and happy riting!

Dr. Cuthbert Soup, PhD